PEN PALS:
SUPER SPECIAL ONE

DREAM
HOLIDAY

———◆———

by Sharon Dennis Wyeth

A YEARLING BOOK

Published by
Dell Publishing
a division of
Bantam Doubleday Dell Publishing Group, Inc.
666 Fifth Avenue
New York, New York 10103

ISBN: 0-440-40395-2

Published by arrangement with Parachute Press, Inc.
Printed in the United States of America
November 1990
10 9 8 7 6 5 4 3 2 1
OPM

For Michelle Poploff and Judy Newman

PART ONE

CHAPTER ONE

VACATION JOURNAL CONTRACT

We the Foxes of the Third Dimension of Suite 3-D, Fox Hall, Alma Stephens School for Girls in Brighton, New Hampshire, do hereby promise to each keep journals at home over the winter holidays. We also promise to share all pen pal letters we receive, no matter how personal.
Signed,

Max Schloss

Shannon Davis

Palmer Durand

Amy Ho

Dear Lisa,
   What do you think of this contract? Neat, huh? Max, Amy, Palmer, and I thought it up when we were talking

about writing to each other over Christmas. Amy figured out that if each one of us wrote the other three every day, that would come to forty-two letters per person over the holiday. Even I can't write forty-two letters in two weeks and of course, that's not even counting the letters I will probably write to Mars! I have to keep writing to him, since he is my pen pal. And of course, I wouldn't dream of not writing to you over the holidays. After all, technically, you are still one of the Foxes of the Third Dimension, even though you're not at Alma this year. By the way, are your parents still separated? I know that you were hoping that they would get back together by Christmas. To keep on the topic of the vacation journals, how about it? At the end of vacation when we come back to school, Max, Amy, Palmer, and I plan to exchange and read each other's journals. Everybody is into it but Palmer, of course. She thinks it's too much work, but we got her to sign the contract by offering a prize to the person who writes the best journal. She can't resist the thought of getting a prize, even though she hates anything to do with writing or spelling.

I have another piece of news. My new roommate Max Schloss (She still seems new to me, even though it's December. Guess I really got used to being in the same room with you, last year.) says that her parents are giving a huge, huge party in New York sometime after Christmas. And Max has asked her parents to let us come! By us I mean the Foxes of the Third Dimension, and that includes you! I've already asked Max about inviting you, in fact. I hope my parents let me go. I'm not sure if I'll be able to come. Going to New York from here in Brighton probably costs a lot of money. Wouldn't it be neat if we were in New York together! It's been so long since I've seen you. Hope we're still best buddies. Please say yes to keeping the journal.

Love,
Shanon

Dear Shanon,
   The idea of the vacation journal and the exchange sounds great! So add my name to the contract. You can even forge my signature! (smile) This will be a good way for us to keep up with each other. I may want to write letters to you also though. I'm glad that you and Mars are still pen pals. So are Rob and I. You're right, it's been a long time since we've seen each other. It's been a long time since I've seen Rob, too. He keeps me supplied with pictures, however, and he's getting cuter and cuter. To answer the question about my parents—yes, they are still separated. Reggie doesn't seem to mind it and doesn't talk about it at all. He's already at home, since Ardsley is out. My last day of school was today. The public schools seem to get out later than the private ones. Max's party sounds super. I hope I do get invited and I do get to go. I really want to see you again, also. Have a Merry Christmas. Tell Amy, Palmer, and Max "Hi!" from me. And tell Max that I hope to meet her someday.

XXX OOO's
Lisa

Vacation Journal, Shanon Davis
Day one

It's great to be home! Everything in my house is so normal! Sometimes I get teased about this, but when I think about Lisa I realize how lucky I am. My mother looks great and so does my dad and so does my grandmother Nana and so do my little brothers Cody, Harry, and Ben and so do my dogs Sallie and Dan! My dad is painting my bedroom. I have shared a bedroom all my life with my big sister, Doreen. Doreen came home from junior college the same day I came home from Alma. Dad wasn't finished painting our room, so we slept in the hallway in our sleeping bags. My sister is so gorgeous! Not only that she is my favorite person. Other sisters I know fight each other, but not me and Doreen. . . .

———————

Vacation Journal, Diary, or whatever . . . by Amy Ho

Sock it to me, baby
It's Christmas all the way
Fry my 'taters, it's Santa in a sleigh . . .

Gotcha, Foxes of the Third Dimension! I bet you thought I was going to write a corny rock and roll song for you on the very first page of this vacation diary, journal, or whatever you want to call it. But I won't. Instead I will tell you that I got home safely from the airport and am home here in New York City, and that already my parents aren't letting me do anything unless I have my big brother along with me! "Can I go to the movies, Mom?" I ask. My mom is in her studio, working on some photographs. "Sure," she calls out to me, "just take Alex!" I go to my dad's office. He has two offices, one in the apartment and one farther downtown in one of his stores. "Hey, Dad," I ask, "can I go across the street to get a new CD?" "As long as you take Alex," Dad answers. Who do they think my brother is, my bodyguard? And who do they think I am, a baby? And Mom and Dad are already on my case about my clothes! Instead of the wardrobe I'm used to wearing, they make me wear these dweeby-looking dresses with bows. I just hope that none of my friends from Alma see me dressed this way! The one thing I want for Christmas is to get my ears pierced. I've only been asking since I was ten! Mom and Dad had better come through.

Vacation Journal—Max Schloss

Okay, it's day one and I'm here in New York. This afternoon I plan to call Amy Elizabeth Ho and see if we can get together in the city. Amy can probably show me a lot of sights here that even I've never seen. I've been thinking about Amy a lot. Of all the girls in Fox Hall, she is definitely the most independent and cool acting. She wears black leather and great hair styles. I guess her parents must give her a lot of freedom. She's probably already got tickets to the Paula Abdul concert. My parents give me an average amount of freedom even though my mom still does pick out my clothes. Unfortunately her taste and my taste are not similar, however, since my mom's into things that are flowered. She always has on flowered dresses and all the slipcovers on the couches are flowered and she tries to make me wear flowered things, too. I've thought about why she is like this and have decided it's because she was once a hippie. Now she's a lawyer, however. Besides my mom, I've got three brothers eight, nine, and ten. Their names are Gary, Brian, and Kevin and they are into acting very dumb. In fact, in secret, I call them the "monster pip-squeaks." Actually, this isn't a secret all that much, since they've heard me calling them that. Last night they put soap in my trombone. That's their idea of being funny.

And my dad is no better when it comes to joking around. After all, *he* acts dumb for a living—doing funny stuff on his television show. Don't get me wrong—even though my mom was once a hippie, and my dad and brothers clown around—I know I have a great family. One of the nicest things about my mom, for example, is the great parties she gives, one of which is coming up and at which I'm hoping to see the Foxes of the Third Dimension.

Oh, yes, VERY IMPORTANT—I got a letter from Jose!

Dear Max,
Do you really believe in Santa Claus? What is the proof?
Your fren,
Jose

That's how he spelled *friend*. I've tried to help him with his spelling, but it's no use. I guess that's what I get for having a kid for a pen pal. Anyway, how am I going to answer this letter? What *is* the proof? . . .

My Christmas Vacation Diary, by Lisa McGreevy

I wonder what kind of Christmas it will be, now that Mom and Dad are not living together. I wonder how it will be on Christmas morning. . . .

Vacation Stupid Journal, by Palmer S. Durand

I am at my mom's home in Palm Beach, Florida, which is a mansion. I like living in a mansion. I saw a cute boy in the country club who looks just like my pen pal Sam O'Leary! At first I thought it was Sam O'Leary! After Christmas here, I am going to California. There I will have a second Christmas with my father. I am partly not looking forward to this, because I will also have to see my stepmother Alicia and my stepsister Georgette. Alicia is not bad, but as you all know from the experience of having her at Alma, Georgette is definitely not nice. The part I am looking forward to is the presents and seeing my dad of course. I should get a lot of gifts. I have made a big list. I hate writing this journal, but I will do it since I am a Fox of the Third Dimension and am curious about what the prize for the best journal will be. I think it should be something in the clothing area. Merry Christmas.

Palmer Durand

CHAPTER TWO

Palmer Durand—My Christmas List

1. A trip to Disneyland for me and three friends I choose.
2. Tennis Raket
3. White socks
4. A maid
5. lipstick and nail polish set (type—"Blossom Pink")
6. Japanese silk bathrobe with my name on it, *Palmer* (I can discribe this more if necesary)
7. Flowers for the rest of my life
8. Scarf
9. Black dress with shiny things on it and no straps Strapless bra (Mom, I really need this! to go with dress)
10. Regular bra (not an undershirt)
11. Gold earrings in shape of large turtles (I'm not sure where I saw these.)
12. Pink tights
13. Money, Money, Money!
14. An electric ice cream maker with a year's supply of ingreedients for chocolate ice cream (zits!)

15. A juicer (For fresh juice in our suite)
16. A pizza cutter (My friends would like this)
17. A jar of instant, real coffee or else peppermint tea bags and a cup with my name on it, *Palmer*
18. Professional modeling lessons (this would be good for me)
19. A computer
20. My own telephone
21. A sports car
22. A bathing suit
23. A new party dress, blue
24. A bigger allowance
25. Some underwear (including bras and not undershirts; I really need this)
26. A waterproof Walkman with a clock, stopwatch, and a calendar
27. Keds
28. Regular shoes, blue; also brown, black, tan, and red
29. boots, black, brown, and light green
30. A pair of ski goggles
31. Plaid skirt
32. Turtlenecks
33. Tickets to Perfect Gentlemen concert (in France)
34. Markers
35. A real sword and fencing lessons
36. A baby sister
37. A BIG surprise!!!

A few weeks before Christmas I made three copies of this list, one for my mother, one for my father, and the other one for my Santa Claus list. I mailed the one for my mother to Palm Beach, Florida; the one for my father to Los Angeles, California; and the one for Santa Claus to the North Pole. I figured I should cover all the bases, hoping that my parents would talk to each other before they bought things so that I wouldn't receive too many duplicates. Santa Claus never seems to duplicate so I didn't worry about him.

Having two Christmases definitely has its advantages, at least as far as the number of presents you receive. Since I was traveling on Christmas Day to see my father, I celebrated Christmas with my mother on Christmas Eve. Mom and I sat around in front of our Christmas tree, which is spectacular, even though it is artificial (my mom is allergic to pine needles), and opened the present I got for her and *all* the gifts I got from her and from the North Pole. First of all, the present I got for my mom was a pair of fuzzy slippers. My mom likes fuzzy things, as long as they are not in the form of dogs and cats, which she is allergic to, and she loved these slippers, which are white and feathery-looking! She gave me a big hug and started to cry a little. (Christmas makes her depressed.) Then I opened my stuff! Of the things on the list, Mom got me numbers 5, 6 (without my name), 8 (in blue), 10, 11 (not sure if these are real gold, but they are turtles), 22, 23, 24, 25, 27, and 32, 34, and 35! By the way, number 36 was a joke, since I know that my mother and father are never going to have children with each other again, since they are divorced. Sure, sometimes I can't help wishing that there was a baby in one of my houses. I never had a baby brother or sister, only my stepsister Georgette who doesn't count because she is not *that* much younger than me and also has an awful personality.

I was on the whole pleased about the presents Mom gave me, especially number ten (the bra), which up until now my mother has refused to understand about. Number twenty-three (the blue party dress) is what I plan to wear to Max's party in New York. Number 24 (bigger allowance) is only five dollars higher and the underwear (number 25), which included a pair of red long johns and a lot of undershirts, I didn't really need that much. I had only written down underwear so that I could repeat that I wanted a real bra in case my mom or dad had missed the point. I think the biggest disappointment of my Palm Beach Christmas is that I did not receive a black dress with shiny things on it and no straps. I did not see a dress like this in a store or a magazine, but on a girl *my age* at my mom's club. My mom and I had a discussion about it, and she said the girl was a lot older than me. I think that girl was exactly my age and that I would look very good in this kind of outfit. Other gifts from my mom that I like are the real sword (which I don't actually have yet) and some fencing lessons. Mom has said that this will be a gift from her this summer. I have always wanted to know how to fence for some reason. This may surprise you, but my first two Halloweens when I was a small child, I dressed up as Zorro. Maybe you haven't heard of Zorro. He is a man in a black mask and cape and has a sword. His show was on television a long, long time ago, but my mom knows about him, and I have seen reruns. Everyone I know would be shocked at this, since I would never wear a boy's costume now. In fact since I turned eight years old, my favorite thing to be has been a princess. But when I was four and five I wanted to be Zorro and have a real sword. And now thanks to my mother, this summer I will actually have a real sword and learn how to fence! My mom's favorite present that she gave me was number 34, the markers. Some people would think this is the most boring gift on the list, but my mom is an artist and loves to give me all kinds of art supplies. These markers are very special colors and come in a beau-

13

tiful box. I like them, too. Though if I had a choice between these markers and the black dress with shiny things,
I would have taken the dress.

My presents from Santa Claus were in Palm Beach also.
The only thing he gave me was shoes and boots though. I
got three pair of shoes (blue, black, and tan) and two pairs
of boots (white rubber and a pair in light green leather).
Santa also gave me a pair of Keds. "I guess the North Pole
must be one great big shoe store!" I joked to my mom on
Christmas morning. That made her laugh a little, but after
a while she looked sad again. My mom gets sentimental on
holidays. In fact all while I was at home, I kept catching
her with a sad look in her eyes. It didn't bother me much
though since she stayed in her room or else just painted in
her studio. Me, I visited a lot of friends and met a very cute
new boy who has blond hair and big blue eyes. In fact, he
looks an awful lot like Sam O'Leary, though he might have
been a little bit taller. He was not a drummer like Sam
O'Leary, but he did know how to dive really well at the
swimming pool. At my friend Lauren's house, we also
played Pictionary and this boy was very good at that, too.
Mainly, he was cute though. If I was in Palm Beach more
I would definitely try to hang out with him, because I'm
sure that he liked me. Even though we didn't speak much
personally, since we were in a group, he always tried to
stand or sit next to me. He also splashed me in the swimming pool. When the time came to leave for L.A., I felt
sorry to leave him, though I remembered that there is a
really cute boy who lives next door to my father's house.
His name is Frankie.

When I said good-bye to my mom at the airport, she
gave me a huge hug and said to hurry back. I felt sad for
a minute. I don't get to spend much time with my mother,
and unlike my father who is married to Alicia, my mom is

14

all alone. I reminded her that I would be coming back again before I go back to Alma.

The airplane ride to L.A. was interesting. I was sitting next to a lady named Mary who was blind. I really didn't notice that she was blind until after we had taken off and she got up to go to the ladies' room. I noticed she needed help from a stewardess in finding her way. But then, I also noticed that she came back all by herself. I wondered how she knew where her seat was. Then I figured out that on her way to the ladies' room she touched and counted each seat she passed. When the stewards and stewardesses came with our food, I watched her feeling around on her tray. She found her knife and fork without any problem and took them out of the wrapper. I think that Mary must have known somehow that I was watching her, even though she couldn't see me, because it was then that she introduced herself and asked me my name. I felt kind of nervous, thinking maybe that I had to speak in a special way to her since she couldn't see me. But after a while I realized that wasn't so. She was nice and asked me a lot of questions about myself and I told her about Sam O'Leary and how I write letters to him. She asked if he was my boyfriend and I said yes, even though it's not totally true. The truth is that I would like him to be my boyfriend. I would like any boy to be my boyfriend, as a matter of fact. Fourteen is definitely old enough as far as I can see. Anyway, the plane ride was not as boring as usual since I was sitting next to Mary. She asked me to tell her what I saw out of the window and I told her. She also asked me to help pour milk into her tea. Then she wanted to know all about school and my family. I told her about mom and dad and my stepmother and Georgette. I didn't exactly say that I hated Georgette, since I didn't think this would be such a cool thing to say to a stranger. But I did tell her about how

15

angry I got the time Georgette tried to kill me by running me over with a wheelbarrow. She was five and I was six and a half and we were both planting little gardens in the yard in California. Georgette was jealous because my flowers were growing taller than hers, so one day while I was watering the garden, she came running down the hill toward me, pushing a wheelbarrow. If my dad hadn't stopped her, I'm sure I would have been killed—run over by a wheelbarrow by my stepsister. After I told Mary this story, she didn't say much. I think she was shocked.

Georgette was at the airport with my dad when he picked me up. I had hoped that she wouldn't be. When I come home to L.A. now, there is never five minutes when my father and I are alone. Ever since Dad adopted Georgette after he married her mother Alicia, it has been just like she is his real daughter. At first it didn't bother me, but now it does. Especially since Georgette has turned out to be such an underhanded person. It also doesn't help that she is always showing off how smart she is. I believe that I might be the only one in the whole world who knows the truth about Georgette. Alicia and my dad think she is perfect. That's why I call her "Miss Perfect" in private.

Miss Perfect managed to ruin things almost as soon as I got there. It all had to do with number 37 on my Christmas list. Number 36 was also a part of it.

Dad and Alicia had planned a very nice dinner for me. I was kind of tired from my airplane flight so I went up to my room, and Dad started up the fire for a barbecue. Even though I really didn't want to be with her, Georgette was hot on my trail.

"So what did you get for Christmas?" she asked, as if that was the only thing in the world that was important.

I told her I got lots of things too numerous to mention, though I did mention the bra and the fencing lessons. Then

16

Georgette sat down on my bed and told me all the things she had gotten. One of them was a black dress with shiny things on it that Alicia had gotten from a thrift store.

"That's exactly what I wanted," I said, screwing my nose up. Where had Georgette gotten the idea to ask for a black dress with shiny things? I decided that she must have seen my Christmas list. A little while later I found out that I was right.

"What made you think of asking for a dress like that?" I asked Georgette.

My sister smiled this really sweet smile she always has when she does something sneaky. "It just popped into my head," she said.

I fooled around with some things on my dresser and Georgette started talking. "I got forty-five presents," she told me.

I almost choked. "Forty-five?" I said. *This is really greedy,* I thought. I only had thirty-seven presents on my whole list and I hadn't gotten half of them. Of course, I hadn't gotten my dad's gifts yet, but I was sure he wasn't going to come up with forty-five of them.

"A lot of them must be little," I told Georgette. "Some of them are hair ornaments, right?"

"A few," said Georgette. She cocked her head sideways and looked at me. "I talked Mom and Dad into giving you your trip to Disneyland," she said.

I was shocked. This was so nice of her! "You did?" I said. "For me and three friends that I choose?"

For some reason Georgette started to blush. "Two or three," she said quickly. "You'll see. They've been planning it."

"Wow," I said. I sat down on my bed. Here I had been thinking that L.A. would be a bummer, but Dad and Alicia were actually planning to take me and two or three of my

17

friends to Disneyland! I started thinking quickly. I would invite Amy, Shanon, and if a third person could make it, it would be Max. Of course, Max was probably busy in New York planning her party. Come to think of it, if I was going to even invite Shanon and Amy to come to L.A., I had to figure out the plans right away, since all of us are going to New York over the vacation. I haven't asked my father about this yet, but I'm sure he'll let me. In fact, Mom has already made the flight arrangements. Maybe it would be better to take my friends to Disneyland over spring vacation instead of Christmas. That would give them time to plan and also ask their parents.

"Thanks for talking Dad and Alicia into giving me that present," I said to Georgette.

"That's okay," said Georgette. "Wait until you see the other stuff they got you."

"You know what it is?" I asked, not liking the idea that she knew everything before me, even what stuff I was getting for Christmas.

"I don't know everything," she said, "but I did make a few recommendations." It's just like my sister to use a word like "recommendations," to make herself sound really intelligent and important. "Thanks a lot," I said, trying to be friendly. After all, Georgette had gotten me the Disneyland trip. "What other things did you get for Christmas?" I couldn't help asking. "Just name a few, not all forty-five of them."

"The big thing is that I'm going to see Perfect Gentlemen," she said. "Mom is going on a business trip to France this spring and that's when they're going to be there."

I could hardly speak I was so shocked. This was on my list, too! And I hadn't gotten it! In fact, I had written it down as a joke. And Georgette was actually going to France with her mother to see one of my favorite groups.

18

"Awesome," I said, trying really hard not to sound jealous. "I didn't know you liked Perfect Gentlemen."

Georgette batted her eyes at me. "Everybody does," she said flatly.

I got up and left the room. I had had enough! I wanted to see my own presents! *After what Georgette had gotten,* I thought, *they had better be great.* Not that I'm as greedy as she is!

"There you are, sweetheart," Alicia said when she saw me. My stepmother is so cheerful and kind, the opposite of my mother, who is also kind, but not too cheerful. "Would you like to open your gifts now or after dinner?"

Dad came into the living room. He had on his barbecue apron and he smelled like charcoal. "The burgers are almost ready," he said, giving me a hug. "Maybe we should eat."

"No, let's open presents," I said, walking over to the Christmas tree. Underneath I spotted the salt and pepper shakers I'd given to Alicia and my father and the "I'd Rather Be Playing Tennis" T-shirt I'd gotten for my father.

"We opened our gifts this morning," my dad said, giving me a kiss. "I hope you don't mind. I love my T-shirt."

"And I like the book you sent me," Georgette chimed in sweetly. She thrust a thin package in my face. "I got one for you, too."

"Thanks," I muttered. There's nothing worse than someone telling you what's inside of a gift they've gotten you.

To be polite I opened Georgette's package. Inside was a diary with blank pages. I wanted to say "I have one of these," but I didn't. "It has a nice cover," I said. "Thanks a lot."

"You're welcome," my stepsister said sweetly.

"Now, let Palmer open her presents from us!" Alicia

said in a cheery voice. She pointed beneath the tree. "All the wrapped things have your name on them," she said, smiling.

"Wow!" I said. "That's a lot of stuff!" I turned to my father. "And Georgette already told me about the Disneyland trip you're giving me!" I said excitedly. "I can't believe how it is that I'm going to be able to take friends!"

"You can do it while you're here," said Alicia.

"I think it might have to wait until spring vacation," I said. "Amy, Shanon, and Max are kind of booked up, and they'd have to ask their parents."

My father looked puzzled. "That's not exactly what we had in mind," he said. "Alicia and I figured that you might invite some friends who live here."

"But I don't have any friends here," I said. "Not many anyway, except Frankie."

Alicia smiled. "That's what Georgette thought, that you and she and Frankie . . ."

"I don't think you understood what was on my Christmas list," I started to argue. "I said that I wanted three friends that I *choose*—"

"You can choose someone who lives here," my dad said gently. "Georgette was thinking that you and Frankie and—"

"This was supposed to be my Christmas present, Dad," I said, "not Georgette's. Anyway, I've been to Disneyland before. I wanted to go with three friends that I choose, not that Georgette—"

"Calm down, Princess," said Dad. "This is one holiday I want you and your sister to get along, okay?"

I looked at my dad and Alicia. They were both smiling these big smiles. I decided for their sake not to get into a fight right away. So for a moment I put the Disneyland trip out of my mind. Besides, there were so many things

20

under the tree with my name on them! In the back I noticed a huge, huge package.

"Open up your goodies!" Georgette said, jumping up and down like a five-year-old.

I sat down on the floor. It felt like my birthday. First there was a hand-painted silk scarf from Alicia. She's painted one of these for me before and they're really beautiful. Then from my dad there was a tennis racket, white socks, pink tights, money (fifty dollars!), a waterproof Walkman with a clock, stopwatch, and a calendar! *This was quite a haul, I thought, if you count in the Disneyland trip, too.* But behind the tree there was still that big one. It was wrapped in shiny red paper with a beautiful golden bow. The box was two feet high, and I was dying to know what was inside of it.

"She saved the best for last," said Georgette.

"You know what's inside?" I said.

"Shhh!" said Alicia. "It's a surprise."

"I hope you like it," said Dad, looking thoughtful. "I kind of let the girls decide on it. . . ."

I pulled the huge box out from behind the tree. It took ages to pull off the paper. I couldn't imagine what was inside. Maybe it was a television! Or a CD player or a stereo system with two tape players, a record player, and AM & FM radio!

What a shock! Inside of the huge box was a huge *doll*. The doll had blond hair and it was wearing a sweater with my name on it, *Palmer*.

At first I couldn't say anything. Dad was smiling and Alicia was smiling, and I think Georgette might have been laughing.

"Don't you like it?" Alicia said, finally.

"Sure," I gulped. I didn't want to be rude. "What is it?" I asked.

21

"Georgette told us you liked dolls," said Alicia. "That you'd become a collector."

I looked at Georgette. "I never said that," I said.

"Don't you remember when we went to that doll hospital near Brighton and you said it was interesting?" Georgette pouted. "You said you wished that you'd collected dolls."

I did not remember this. I did stop at the doll hospital with Georgette and her roommate Tina Penderhew. I may have said that the dolls were interesting, but I would never have asked for a doll for Christmas!

"Some girls still like dolls," Dad said. He looked disappointed.

"It's fabulous!" I said, trying to sound cheerful. I patted the doll on the head. "How did you think of the idea of having a sweater with my name on it?"

"Georgette gave me the idea," said Alicia.

I picked up my waterproof Walkman. This is something I liked.

"Let's go eat!" Dad said, putting an arm around me.

"I'll get the salad," said Alicia.

"I don't care if you don't like the doll," Georgette said huffily. "I think she's cute."

Our dinner outside was nice. I peeked over the fence to see Frankie, but he wasn't there.

"Is Frankie home for the holiday?" I asked.

"He's here all right!" Georgette said with a giggle. "I talked with him all morning."

Uh-oh, I thought. Frankie's was the one place I thought of to get away from my stepsister. She had never liked Frankie before. But if he and she were friends now . . .

"Merry Christmas, everybody," said my father.

Alicia and he clinked glasses and then he clinked my

glass, too. No matter what presents I got, I was glad to be with my father.

"Merry Christmas," I said, smiling at Dad.

That night, Georgette knocked on the door of my room. "I thought I was doing something nice when I told them to get the doll," she said.

"It wasn't on my list," I couldn't help saying.

"Yes, it was," she said. "Number thirty-seven."

I tried to think what number thirty-seven was.

"A big surprise," Georgette reminded me, smiling.

"Hey, I thought you said you hadn't read my list," I told her. My stepsister is always lying.

"Well, I had only read it once," she said.

"Maybe I can find somebody who actually is a doll collector," I said, trying to be pleasant. "Of course, they'll wonder why the doll's name is Palmer."

Georgette smiled at me. "Thanks for the book," she said. "I read it in an hour."

"Just like that, huh?" I said. Reading a whole book takes me about two weeks.

"The vocabulary's quite simple," Georgette informed me.

"I'll remember that the next time I go book shopping for you," I said, trying not to be grouchy. I opened up my suitcase and unpacked my underwear, making sure Georgette saw my new bra. This was kind of a mean thing to do since she doesn't wear one.

"How come you want a new sister?" she blurted out.

"Huh?" I said. Now what was she talking about?

"Number thirty-six on your list said you wanted a new sister," Georgette insisted. She was pouting and looked as if her feelings were hurt.

"I certainly didn't mean that I wanted to get rid of you," I told her. Of course this is not quite the truth, but since it

23

was the Christmas season I didn't want to be too cruel about it.

"I'm the only sister you have," said Georgette. "When you wrote down that you wanted a new one—"

"Is that why you did that sneaky thing and told Dad and Alicia that I was a doll collector?" I asked her. That had to be it! Seeing that I had asked for a "new sister" on the list, Georgette had gotten insulted. "Were you trying to get me back?" I asked. "Is that why you 'recommended' the doll?"

"Certainly not," Georgette said, wiggling out. "I'm not a rat, you know." She stood there in her white lace night-gown just like the one I have. My sister has the appearance at least of a really sweet person.

"Forget about the doll," I said generously. "The thing on my list about the sister was a joke. You'll notice I said 'new baby sister.' It's a joke, since nobody in our family is going to have any more kids."

"Dad and Mom still might," said Georgette.

The thought hadn't really occurred to me, since Georgette was twelve and Dad and Alicia hadn't had any more. And at the moment, I didn't feel much like thinking about it. "It was a stupid thing to put down on the list," I told Georgette. "Are you satisfied?"

"I guess," she said, smiling. She sat down on my bed again and started swinging her feet. I don't think Georgette likes me, so it beats me why she hangs around me so much. "What do you want to do tomorrow?" she asked.

"Oh, I don't know . . ." I answered, thinking I'd sneak over to Frankie's.

"Frankie and I are going to play Monopoly," Georgette told me, batting her eyes.

"Cool," I muttered, thinking how definitely uncool I thought it was. So that's the way my California Christmas started.

CHAPTER THREE

Dear Palmer
  Today my sister asked me if I had a girlfriend and I said yes that my girlfriend was you. I hope you don't mind. Let me know what you think. I hope you are enjoying your California Christmas.

Love,
Sam

Being Sam O'Leary's girlfriend is what I have been dreaming of ever since I met him last year and we became pen pals! I can't believe it has finally happened. As soon as I saw a letter from him in the mailbox outside my father's house, I was so excited I thought I'd go crazy. I didn't even mind that much that every minute of my time here has been spent with Georgette, and that Georgette insists on hanging around Frankie. Let my little sister hang around Frankie if she wants to. I have a real boyfriend. As soon as I read Sam's letter, I went right away to find Georgette— not to make her jealous, but to share the good news. Georgette was in the backyard hanging over the fence talking to Frankie, who was on his patio, reading a comic book. She was talking about crossword puzzles of all the boring things. Why would a boy as cute as Frankie care about crossword puzzles? My little sister has a lot to learn.

"Excuse me," I said to Georgette. I looked over the fence and smiled at Frankie. He really is cute, even though he's short. I suppose what he sees in Georgette is that all their lives they've lived next door to each other. "I have something private to discuss with you," I told my sister.

Georgette gave me a face that said "Don't bother me, I'm busy," but I pulled her away.

"Stop dragging me," she said when we got to the other side of our yard. "What's so important? Can't you see I was talking to Frankie?"

"I thought you didn't like Frankie," I teased her. "You said he wasn't intellectual enough."

"He still gets horrible grades," Georgette said with a smile, "but I don't care about that anymore."

"Come off it," I teased. "You're little Miss Perfect when it comes to grades."

"I didn't say I don't care about *my* grades," she said. "I don't care what kind of grades Frankie gets." She batted her eyes and grinned over her shoulder. "I used to not like boys. Now I do, and I think that Frankie is very charismatic."

I rolled my eyes. Only Georgette would use the word "charismatic" to describe somebody who reads comic books. "Frankie's cute," I admitted, pulling Sam's letter out of my pocket, "but not as cute as my boyfriend!"

"Since when do you have a boyfriend?" said Georgette.

"Since I got this letter," I told her. I took Sam's letter out and read it. I think I saw Georgette actually turn green. Ever since she started going to school with me at Alma Stephens, she's been asking all kinds of questions about my

26

pen pal. I'm sure she likes him and wishes Sam were her boyfriend.

"What are you going to write back?" Georgette asked.

"Definite *yes*," I said, smiling. "Sam O'Leary is the cutest boy I know!"

"He's not that cute," grumbled Georgette.

I couldn't believe how jealous she was. Why couldn't she be happy about my good news? "Sam is very cute and you know it," I told her.

"Cute is not everything," she said. "Sam doesn't go to Ardsley."

"Who cares about Ardsley?" I said angrily.

"All the girls at Alma do," said Georgette. "The Ardies are much cooler than the boys at Sam's school."

"Well, Frankie doesn't go to Ardsley," I argued, "and you think he's charismatic."

"Frankie doesn't have to go to Ardsley," Georgette said spitefully, "because he lives in California."

"I don't know why I wasted my time even telling you about Sam," I said, feeling furious. "I should have known you would just act jealous."

"Why should I be jealous because you've got a boyfriend?" said Georgette. "Besides, you're jealous that Frankie's my friend and not your friend."

I glared at her. Then we both looked over our shoulders. Luckily Frankie had gone inside. Now we could really argue.

"You're jealous of the fifty dollars Dad gave me!" I said. "Dad may have given you a thousand gifts, but he didn't give you any money."

"That's because he gave me a charge card," Georgette announced triumphantly. "He gave you one, and you abused the privilege by charging too much!"

27

"I didn't abuse anything!" I shouted. "Not only that, you got the idea for the black dress with shiny things from my Christmas list!"

"More than one person can get the idea to want a black dress!" Georgette shouted.

Alicia came out. "What's the problem here?" she asked. Even though Georgette and I were fighting, Alicia was still trying to sound cheerful.

"I shared a personal letter with Georgette, and she started shouting at me," I said.

"Not true," said Georgette. "I was having a nice time with Frankie, and she dragged me away. Now Frankie's gone inside and it's Palmer's fault."

Alicia suggested that we both go to our rooms separately to cool off. She said that tomorrow there was going to be a surprise. I hoped that it wasn't going to be another doll wearing a sweater with my name on it. When Georgette and I got to the top of the stairs, we were so angry with each other, we weren't talking. But instead of going into our rooms, we just stood there and glared.

"You're jealous because you're not invited to Max Schloss's party," I said, zinging her one last time.

Georgette batted her eyes and looked as if she was going to cry. Bragging about a great party she wasn't invited to might have been hitting below the belt. Even though I felt bad for a moment, I didn't apologize. Instead I went into my room, slammed the door, and wrote a letter to Sam O'Leary.

Dear Sam,

Definite yes to what you asked me. I do not mind!! Actually, I like it. Hope you are having a happy Christmas. At the moment I am having difficulties with my sister, who is very jealous of me and a pest. Soon, however, I will be

*going to New York for a party at Max's house and then
back to Florida for the end of vacation. Thanks again for
asking me what you did!*

> *With much love,*
> *Palmer*
> *(Your girlfriend)*

I just noticed that I have written a lot in my journal. I
didn't think I'd like writing in it, but it isn't *that* bad.

Well, Dad and Alicia did give me a trip to Disneyland,
but as I kind of figured out on that first day, it wasn't the
way I had wanted it. When Dad told me that he hadn't
intended to have me invite three friends from out of town
to go with me, I was truly disappointed. When he realized
how bummed out I was, he did promise that he would
think about doing something like inviting one friend from
school to L.A. in the future and taking us to Disneyland.

Naturally, Georgette managed to wheedle her way into
my present. The three "friends" I took to Disneyland
turned out to be Georgette, Frankie, and my stepmother
Alicia. I tried to get another girl I used to know who lives
in L.A., but she couldn't come with us. If this had been last
year when Frankie seemed to like me and I liked him, this
Disneyland trip wouldn't have been so bad. But since Georgette has done nothing but hang around with Frankie all
vacation and talk his ear off, the two of them might as well
have been "dates." When we got to Tomorrowland, it was
unbelievable the way Georgette grabbed Frankie's hand
and almost pushed him into one of those little sports cars
you can drive around in. Of course, there was room in the
car for only two people, so I was left standing there with
Alicia. I suppose I could have figured out that Georgette
was going to hog Frankie on the rides and jumped in front
of her before they got into the car, but that would have

29

been so pushy and immature. I decided I would do it the next time, maybe when we went to Adventureland.

"Want to drive one of those cars?" Alicia asked.

"No thanks," I said.

My stepmother touched me on the shoulder. "Having fun?"

"Not really," I admitted. The fact was that I wished that Dad had been able to come. I was also getting tired of competing with my stepsister over everything.

"I hope you're not feeling left out," Alicia said. "Frankie and Georgette seem to have gotten closer."

"They used to hate each other," I said with a laugh.

"They go through phases," Alicia said with a knowing nod. "After all, all their lives they've lived next door to each other."

"Frankie knows me, too, though," I said. "He and I used to talk a lot whenever I'd come here."

Alicia winked. "Why don't you go on the next ride with him?"

I giggled. Sometimes I like my stepmother. We sat down on a bench to wait for Georgette and Frankie.

"Did you like your Christmas gifts?" Alicia asked.

"Don't mean to be rude," I said, "but I hate the doll."

"Sorry about that," said Alicia. She touched my hair a little. "How are things in Florida?" she asked. "How is your mother?"

I thought about my mom, the way she felt sentimental about Christmas. "She might be lonely without me," I told Alicia.

"Why don't you and your dad call her tonight?" she suggested.

"Great!" I said. I thought Mom would like that, especially if Dad got on the line. Even though they weren't married anymore, they still cared about each other.

30

"You and Dad are going to let me go to my friend's party in New York, aren't you?" I asked, changing the subject. "Dad said he would think about it."

"I think your father will let you go," said Alicia.

"It's very important to me," I said. "My suitemates are all going to be there."

"We'll work it out," said Alicia, giving my shoulder a squeeze, "even though Eric and I hate to give you up a few days earlier."

I looked at her. Alicia is very pretty and looks a lot like my mom. She also looks a lot like me—in fact, just like Georgette does. "I've had a good time," I said. She and Dad really had been trying. It wasn't their fault that Georgette was such a pain.

"We love you," Alicia said, hugging me. "Eric and I are lucky to have *two* beautiful daughters."

Though what she said was mushy, it also made me feel good. It was nice to know that Alicia thinks of me as her daughter.

The rest of the afternoon turned out okay. Alicia and I talked some more, and Georgette and I didn't fight as much, even though I did manage to bump her a few times and ride next to Frankie. My stepsister and I even took a few rides together while Frankie rode with Alicia.

The conclusions I reached at the end of my California Christmas are these: that I love my dad and he loves me, that Alicia is kind, and that Georgette is the pest she always was.

CHAPTER FOUR

Vacation Journal—Max Schloss

This is the journal of Maxine Edith Schloss. I am upstairs in my cave, writing. Actually, I'm in my room, but I'm trying to be dramatic for the benefit of my friends who will be reading this. The walls of my room are painted dark blue. I have flags of different countries in the windows for curtains. All of this was my idea, but my mom had it carried out by a decorator. On the ceiling there are stars painted that glow in the dark and on one wall there is the mural of a tiger. You will get to see all of this when you come to my party.

Last night we celebrated Hanukkah, and my dad gave us all hand buzzers. My brothers liked them (of course) and kept shaking each other's hands for hours. I pretended not to like the buzzer, but it is pretty funny. Leave it to my dad to give us something dumb like that. Each of the hand buzzers was all wrapped up in a little velvet jewelry box with a blue ribbon. What a joker! He also gave us each twenty-five dollars. Twenty-five dollars is a lot of money for the three pip-squeaks. (And for me!)

For a Hanukkah gift for me, my mom gave me a new dress. It looks just like something she would wear. It is very expensive and flowered and has ribbons and lace on the collar. It looks like something someone would wear to a square dance. It is definitely something from her hippie days. Where does my mom get her taste?

You might think that with Hanukkah *and* Christmas being celebrated in my house and my parents' big party coming up, all I would have had on my mind are celebrations. But that's not quite true. The biggest thing I've had on my mind is Jose. After I got his letter, I really thought a lot. Telling about Santa was a big responsibility. This is what I finally wrote back to him.

Dear Jose,

The answer is yes. I do believe in Santa Claus. For years he has been giving me presents, even though in my house I also celebrate Hanukkah. He fills up my stocking with nuts and oranges and does the same for my brothers. Once when I was three years old, I actually saw him. I was half-asleep, and my mom came to get me. She whispered, "Wake up, Max! I see Santa Claus!" It was like a dream. I was in my pajamas. I used to wear that kind that your little sister wears—the kind with the feet. I sneaked behind our living-room door with my mother. We didn't live in a big house then, we lived in a little apartment. Santa was standing by the window near the fire escape. I heard him talking to himself, while he filled up my stocking. "And this is for little Maxie Schloss," I actually heard him say with my own ears. It was an experience that I've never forgotten. To tell you the truth, I was kind of scared. Seeing Santa Claus on Christmas Eve is kind of like seeing some kind of king or hero or something. I was so scared I started to cry. My mother told me to hush and took me

33

back to bed. I hope this is proof enough to answer your question. This is an eyewitness account. I don't think I've ever told anyone else this story. Of course, the real proof is in all the good things that happen at Christmas. Santa is very generous if you're a good person. So tell Lila and Becky and Billy to be real good. And tell your mom and dad I said "hello." Have a Merry Christmas and Happy Hanukkah.

Love,
Max

I hope this letter is good enough. Everything in it was true. I hope Jose and his family have really nice holidays. They have had a lot of hard times. I hope that Santa comes through for them.

This morning I was feeling sorry for myself. My mom says I am a girl who has everything. Maybe she is right. I definitely got a load of stuff for Hanukkah. My grandmother and grandfather gave me money too, so I have sixty-five dollars, which I might put toward a pair of new Reebok Pumps. But even with the sixty-five dollars, I was still feeling sorry for myself. Money and presents are not everything. Your family paying attention to you counts for a lot, too. Like this morning . . .

When I woke up, I went down to the kitchen for breakfast. Right away, I noticed there were four half-eaten bowls of cereal on a tray on the sideboard. They belonged to Dad, Gary, Brian, and Kevin. I couldn't believe it! We were supposed to go skating. But they'd gotten up early and had gone without me.

Then my mom came downstairs. I wondered what she was doing at home. She usually goes to the office pretty early. But she was still in her terry-cloth bathrobe. *Why doesn't she get a new bathrobe?* I thought. And if I looked as tired as she did, I really wouldn't walk around without makeup!

"Why are you slamming your toast plate around, Maxie?" she asked me.

"I'm not slamming it around," I said.

"Are you angry about something?" Mom asked.

There was no use saying I wasn't mad. She could definitely tell that I was. "Dad left me," I squawked.

"Is that all?" said Mom.

I slammed across the room and got some juice. "What do you mean, is that all?"

"You were sound asleep, sweetie," said Mom. "The boys really wanted to go skating. I suggested to Dad that he let you sleep in. You were out so late last night with your friends. Besides, this morning I thought you and I could go shopping."

"Aren't you going to work?" I asked in surprise.

My mom smiled. "Not until later," she answered. "Meanwhile, I thought we girls could spend some time together," she said.

I rolled my eyes a little bit. Not that I don't like my mother. I do. But it gives me the creeps when she calls us "the girls."

"Don't you want to go shopping?" she asked. Mom poured herself a cup of coffee. She looked kind of hurt.

"What kind of shopping did you have in mind?" I asked, knowing how different our taste in clothes is.

"Underwear and sheets for your bed at school," Mom answered promptly.

"Yuk," I said. "How about some new Reebok Pumps?"

"If you want those, you have to buy them yourself, Maxie," my mom said. My mother is so weird! She spends a fortune on the stuff she wants for me. But when I ask her

35

for something like the Reeboks, she makes me pay for it. I guess this comes from her hippie days. Even though we have enough money, she thinks this is good for me.

"I don't want to go shopping, then," I said stubbornly. I bit into my toast, which was now cold.

Mom looked hurt again. "I suppose you do have a lot of things," she said. "How do you like the dress I got you for a Hanukkah present?"

I looked guilty. I couldn't lie to her, could I? "It has too many flowers," I mumbled.

"I guess you'd rather have something less far out," said my mother.

"I saw a dress that I really like," I said rapidly. "It's red and green plaid with puffy sleeves."

"That dress in that store on Madison Avenue?" my mother asked. "Oh, Maxie. I saw it, too. It's so overpriced, and red doesn't really look good on redheads."

"It was red and green," I said, glaring at the table. "I guess you're not going to buy it for me?"

"Not today," said Mom.

"We don't like the same kind of clothes," I said. "Even though you're a lawyer, you dress like a hippie."

"I'll take that as a compliment," she said, rising.

I got up really fast and tried to change the subject. I almost knocked my juice over. I knew I had hurt my mother's feelings.

"Hey, Mom, wait up," I said. "I have something to ask you."

She looked at me and scrunched up her eyes. "Yes?"

"Uh, do you believe in Santa Claus?" I asked. "It's for a friend that I'm asking."

"I believe in the spirit of Santa Claus," she answered. "I think you're aware of that."

I smiled. I like it when my mom talks like a lawyer.

36

"Once I saw Santa when I was three," I said. "Do you remember that?"

My mother smiled. "I remember," she said softly. Then she touched me on the head. "Sorry your dad and I changed the plans without consulting you," she said.

"That's okay," I said. "It felt good to sleep."

"If you really don't want to go shopping, I'll go into the office," Mom said.

"I don't really need anything," I said. "I think I'll see if Amy is free."

"Good idea," said Mom on her way up the stairs. "I can hardly wait to meet your new school friends!"

I walked down the hall to the living room. In our hallway we have these old suits of armor. And the telephone in the living room is in the shape of a race car. The armor and the race car telephone are my dad's taste. All the flowered slipcovers on everything are my mother's. I sat down on the couch and called Amy.

Somebody answered the phone. "Ho residence. . . ."

I could hardly recognize the voice it was so soft, but something told me that it was Amy. "Do you have a cold, Amy?" I asked.

"Is that you, Max?" Amy sounded really happy to hear from me.

"It's me," I said. "How about going out? Maybe dropping in at the Hard Rock?" I made my voice sound like I'd been there before. "I've got sixty-five dollars," I said, "and that's only from Hanukkah."

There was silence. "Just a minute," said Amy, putting her hand over the phone. I could hear some muffled voices in the background. "I can't go," she said, coming back on again.

"Why not?" I asked.

"Because my brother is busy . . . I mean, uh, I'm busy.

37

That's what I meant to say—I'm too busy to go to the Hard Rock."

"Wow . . . too bad," I said. "Are you coming to the party? My parents are asking my cousin Rain to do the music for us, and he's awesome. Rain's not to be missed."

"I'll definitely make it, one way or the other," she promised.

We said good-bye and hung up. I thought Amy had sounded mysterious. Or maybe she was just having too good a time to talk to me. Imagine being too busy to go to the Hard Rock! She'd probably been there a hundred times already and I'd only been once. I went upstairs to my cave again. My mom poked in her head. She was dressed up for the office. My poor mother!—even in her lawyer suit she looked like a hippie. She had on these gross red beads and a purple flowered blouse. And on her head she was wearing the craziest hat—a black beret covered with metal things. I wanted to suggest that she go change right that minute—at least take off that hat. But I kept my mouth shut. I'd hurt her feelings enough for one day.

"Dad and the boys should be back before lunch," she said. "Maybe you should go ice skating this morning with someone else."

"Good idea," I said. "Amy's busy. I'll call up Juliette. Hey, Mom—" I said, "are you sure that wasn't Dad in a Santa Claus outfit that time when I was three?"

"I swear," my mom said seriously.

"But Dad has a Santa Claus suit," I argued. "He wore it last year."

"He only has that for parties, Maxie," my mother said, smiling. "He wouldn't impersonate someone as important as Santa Claus to fool his children."

I thought for a minute. "I hope that Dad's not going to

wear that Santa suit at this year's party. I've got Amy, Palmer, and Shanon coming."

"You never know with your father," Mom said cheerfully. She blew me a kiss, and I blew one back. Even though I hate her clothes, I love my mother!

But I love my father even better.

CHAPTER FIVE

Max's Journal

For Christmas my mom really surprised me. She gave me the green and red plaid dress with puffy sleeves that I'd been longing for. I'm going to wear it to the party! It's to die for! My parents truly are complicated. The minute I think I have them all figured out, they do something I didn't expect. Like today when my brothers were bowling, my dad canceled this meeting he had with a writer just to be with me.

It was great to be alone in the house with him. For lunch he made one of his special sandwiches. The sandwiches my dad makes are so big, you can hardly wrap your mouth around them. Of course, my mom says they are very unhealthy, and I know that she's right. But Dad and I don't care. My dad's sandwich, which he calls a "Maxie" after his name and also mine, consists of:

A big bun	Tomatoes
Two hamburgers	Fried green peppers
Cheddar cheese	Onions
Mozzarella cheese	Fried eggs

Believe me, this is NOT gross! In fact, this sandwich is served at a very famous delicatessen and on the menu it has my father's name!

"How about we have Maxie sandwiches for the party?" Dad asked when we were in the kitchen making our lunch.

"Great," I said. "Only a lot of people might not want the eggs. Palmer hates eggs."

"We'll have other stuff, too," said my dad with a wink. "Let's you and I plan the menu!" He started smoking a cigar while he was cooking. He only smokes cigars when my mom isn't around. "First of all—how about pizza with chili and raw onions?"

"Excellent," I said with a giggle. "And everyone will have whole fried chickens!"

"We'll have the caterer whip some up," Dad promised.

"How about some ten-foot-long hoagies?" I asked. "Gary, Brian, and Kevin like those."

"Hoagies it will be," said Dad, flipping the eggs.

"Hot dogs and fries, too!" I said, laughing. "And corn on the cob and marshmallows!"

"And while we're at it, we'll have a big bowl of spaghetti," Dad added, chuckling.

"And lobster!" I added, snitching some cheese.

"Good," said Dad. "The boys will like that."

My father and I burst out laughing. Of course we both knew that this menu was ridiculous. My mother was the one who handled those kinds of things. And for a big party like this, she was sure to have a caterer making loads of fancy food.

"What do you think Mom will think about our menu?" Dad asked with a twinkle in his eyes. He loves to make my mom crazy.

I nodded. "She'll think it's too much. But try to get her

41

to have at least one thing that my friends like. Kids don't like caviar."

"I don't like caviar, either," said Daddy. "I'll make sure your mother puts the hoagies on the menu. I like those."

I smiled. "Thanks for letting me invite my friends."

"I can hardly wait to meet them," Dad said with a twinkle in his eye. "Maybe I should tell them a few jokes," he teased.

"Don't do it, Dad," I warned. One of my father's favorite things was razzing my friends. "Some of my old friends might understand you, but Amy, Palmer, and Shanon have never met you before."

"All right, I'll be good," he promised.

"And please don't dress up as Santa Claus," I asked him.

"Scout's honor," Dad said.

I sat back and ate my sandwich. There's an art to eating the "Maxie." If you're not careful, the eggs and the ketchup leak out.

The monster pip-squeaks ran into the kitchen, followed by Ollie, our chauffeur. They threw their parkas all over the floor.

"Hey, I smell sandwiches!" yelled Gary.

"Look, Dad," Brian said, pointing to a box he was carrying that had holes punched in it. "We bought some frogs!"

"Frogs?" I said. "How come?"

"Where did you get them?" Dad asked curiously.

"At the pet store," said my youngest brother, Kevin. "It's right next door to the bowling alley."

"Don't you have enough pets with that snake of yours?" I asked. My brothers are very fond of things that creep and crawl.

"I suggested that they might ask their parents' permission first," Ollie told my dad formally.

42

"It's okay, Ollie," Dad said to the chauffeur. "Never enough pets in my house."

"That's what I say!" yelled Gary. "Come on!" he called to Brian and Kevin. "Let's put them in the terrarium!"

The pip-squeaks thundered out of the kitchen, and Ollie followed them. My dad watched them leave with a big grin on his face.

"Maybe we'll get lucky and the snake will eat the frogs," I suggested.

"Come now, Max," said my father. "Be a good sport."

"There's three of them and one of me," I argued. "They're always ganging up on me. I still haven't got the soap out of my trombone."

"Be patient," my dad said. "They'll grow up—someday."

"I certainly hope they behave themselves at the party," I sulked, dumping my plate in the sink. "How many people are coming to the party, anyway?" I asked.

"About a hundred," Dad replied. "Your mom's keeping the list. I lost count."

"That's a lot of people," I said with a whistle.

Dad chuckled. "The more the merrier!"

I thought for a moment. "There's one more person I wish I could invite, but I guess it's too late now."

"Who is it?" Dad wanted to know.

"His name is Jose," I said. I smiled and thought about the Hurt family. I hoped that they had a nice Christmas.

CHAPTER SIX

Amy's Journal

Yesterday I wrote a song that says how I have been feeling since I came home for the holidays.

ALONE IN MY TOO QUIET HOUSE
Terrible two's, terrible teens
I keep my shout shut, oh, where is my thunder?
While you feel the breeze, I only sneeze
A matter of gender? I guess!
Telling you now, though—I won't rest
Till I feel my might, get to stay out all night
Get to know who I am, not read about it
Get to make myself known, not the quiet voice of home
Girls—we are! And East or West, we are all right!
Terrible two's, terrible teens—just my lonely voice
In the night! In my too quiet house.

All I wanted for Christmas was to have my ears pierced. And my parents did not let me do it. Not only that, a couple of days ago, Max called me up and asked if I wanted to go to the Hard Rock Cafe. My parents made me say no, because Alex couldn't go with me. He had somewhere else to go with some friend of his, probably Jasmine. It was so embarrassing. How could I tell Max that my parents don't trust me enough to let me go to the Hard Rock Cafe with her? Max has probably been there ten times. That's the way she sounded over the telephone. So I told her that I was too busy. She probably thinks I have tons of other fun things planned to do today in the city, but that is far from the truth. The entire vacation has been made up of visits to my relatives, and every time I ask to go somewhere by myself my parents have something else planned for me or just won't let me go. Alex, on the other hand, got a motorcycle for Christmas and has been going everywhere with his girlfriend Jasmine. People might think that Alex has more freedom because he is older than I am, but a couple of years ago when he was my age, my parents let him do lots more things than they allow me. The reason is that he's a boy!

If I were the boy in my family and could do whatever I want to, I certainly wouldn't take advantage of the situation the way my brother does. Even though my parents give Alex a specific time to be home when he goes out, he always comes in two hours later. Then after my dad hollers at him, Alex just does the same thing again. And my parents let him do it! If Alex were my son, he would be grounded. If I were the parent in this family, I would give the freedom to the girl in the house. I would give the freedom to me! I never cause Mom and Dad any trouble. I even wear the dweeby clothes they buy for me when I'm at home. Alex doesn't even wear a necktie when we go out to a restaurant or a jacket either, for that matter. He always ends up leaving it at home accidentally on purpose. It really embarrasses my father when we go to these fancy

45

places to eat and Alex has to borrow a jacket in order to be seated. And yet Mom and Dad never let me go anywhere in the city without Alex to protect me. I'm the one who should protect him, he's so wild and crazy. Why can't my parents see that the one who deserves the freedom in the house is me?

My cousin Ping came over today and Mercedes Hernandez, a girl from my old school. We played cards and looked at videos. I told them all about John and the other Foxes and the pen pals. They thought the idea of the Pen Pal Exchange we have in our suite at Alma was cool. Ping is interested in setting up an exchange like that in her school. She was even more interested after I showed her John's latest letter.

Dear Amy,
   Here's a poem dedicated to you:
         Dressed in black
         Bodacious lady
         Be cool
         Range free
         Like the wild winter night.

                    Love,
                    John

"Wow," said Mercedes, looking at John's letter. "He called you 'bodacious lady'! This guy must be awesome."

"He's a preppy type," I admitted, "but John's okay. I do dig his poetry."

"How come he called you bodacious?" my cousin Ping asked with a puzzled expression on her face. "That doesn't really sound like you. You're so quiet."

I didn't like what my cousin said, but in a way she was right. Around my house, I am quiet. Too quiet. If I said what was really on my mind, my parents would hate it.

"John has a different image of me," I tried to explain to Ping. "He knows me from school."

"In school you're different?" said Ping. Ping is only eleven. And even though I do like her, she's definitely dense at times.

"I hang out with people who are into music at school," I said to my cousin.

"Still write rock 'n' roll?" Mercedes asked, remembering from a couple of years ago.

"It's my favorite hobby," I answered.

"I've got tickets for the Janet Jackson concert!" Ping announced. "You should get some!"

"I tried to," I said glumly, "or at least Alex tried to and I was hoping he would get a ticket for me, too, but the concert was already sold out."

The three of us played cards and watched *Back to the Future II*. I was feeling slightly bummed out. Alex had been out all morning on his motorcycle. I like Ping and it was fun seeing Mercedes, but I wanted to be *out* in the city—not locked in my room watching tapes. Before Mom had gone to her photography studio I'd suggested that Ping, Mercedes, and I might go to a movie uptown but she said no.

"I don't think it's wise for you girls to wander around by yourselves in the street," Mom told me.

I didn't even bother asking my dad if I could go out. He's even more conservative than my mom, so I knew that his answer would be no. He had left very early for his office anyway.

After *Back to the Future II* was over, Mercedes wanted to check out my closet. I'd already shown them my Christmas presents. Since the only one in the loft besides us was the housekeeper, who likes rock 'n' roll, I put on a Paula

Abdul tape and played it full volume. Playing Paula Abdul full volume is something I'd definitely not do if my parents were home.

"I love this jacket!" said Mercedes, pulling out my black leather motorcycle jacket.

"It's old," I said. "It used to belong to Alex and he gave it to me."

"You have the prettiest, frilliest dresses!" Ping said, pointing to the stuff jammed at the other end of the closet.

It figures my cousin liked the dweeby wardrobe my parents picked out for me. "You can have them," I muttered. "The only time I wear them is when I'm home."

"What do you wear at school then?" Ping asked.

"I wear skirts and blouses to class," I explained, "because it's a rule. But as soon as I get back to the suite, I wear this kind of stuff." I pulled out a black spandex jumpsuit hanging next to the motorcycle jacket.

"Cool!" said Mercedes.

"Strange," said Ping. "Do your parents let you wear it?"

"Are you kidding?" I said. "If I wore something like this at home, my father would have a fit. Then when he recovered he'd get really mad at me. I save my cool wardrobe for when I'm going out."

"Why are your parents so strict with you?" Mercedes asked sympathetically. "Your brother Alex's style is definitely outrageous."

"That's Alex," I muttered, "not me. . . ."

When my cousin and my friend left, I put on the black spandex jumpsuit just for fun and experimented with hair styles. Now that my hair is long, it's hard to do anything cool with it. I moussed it back a lot though and did a side ponytail. Then I settled back on the bed with my Walkman and listened to Joan Jett. It was kind of humiliating admitting to Ping and Mercedes that I was *so* obedient to my

48

parents. It's like being two people—a cool person at school and a total nerd at home. But that's always the way I've been, I guess. My parents really do love me, so I try not to do anything to make them mad, even though I'm mad about the way they treat me . . . picking my clothes for me . . . not letting me get my ears pierced . . . never letting me go anywhere by myself. . . . But since Alex is so outrageous I'd better be normal or my mom and dad would probably have nervous breakdowns!

I got up from my bed, still wearing my Walkman, and looked out at the street from my window. We live in downtown Manhattan in a large loft. On our street there are lots of stores and art galleries and interesting people. I wanted to be down there, checking out all those places and people. But I knew I'd better not leave the loft without permission. *Besides, Alex would be home soon,* I thought. Even though I was mad that my brother had more freedom than I had, he was still company. I sat on my dresser and took a look around my room. Every time I left for school, Mom "neat-ened" it up, which meant she made it look like nobody lived there. Over Thanksgiving I'd put up a Madonna poster, but now it was gone. At least there was a little mess in the corner, where I'd piled up my Christmas gifts. I got some nice ones—Alex gave me a black leather knapsack, which is my favorite. My dad gave me a neat book on science and Mom gave me one of her photographs. It was a beautiful beach scene with a crane standing by itself on the shore. I decided to hang it up in my room at school along with that old Madonna poster. . . . Christmas was fun. We went to my uncle's restaurant for dinner, and Ping and some of my other cousins were there. If only I'd been able to have my ears pierced. . . .

I took off my Walkman and flopped down on my pil-lows. I looked at the clock. I'd have to change out of my jumpsuit and put on a dress before dinner. I picked up my guitar and started another verse to my song . . . ALONE IN MY TOO QUIET HOUSE. Then Alex finally came home. He stood at the door listening to me.

"Nice lyrics," he said.

"Thanks a lot," I grumbled. I was so bored and jealous of him because he'd been out all day. "Where did you go with Jasmine?" I asked.

"The Hard Rock Cafe," he answered.

Why did he have to say the Hard Rock? "Lucky you," I said to Alex. "Maybe when I'm twenty-five Mom and Dad will let me go. Maybe they'll let me have my ears pierced then, too."

"Sorry you're so bummed out," my brother said. Alex really is a likable person, but just at the moment he looked so *free* in his new motorcycle jacket, I could have slugged him.

"Leave me alone," I said, picking up my guitar again. "I'm busy."

"No problem," said Alex. "I have to go call Christie, anyway."

"Christie?" I said. "I thought Jasmine was your girl-friend."

"She is," Alex said with a shrug, "but I still like Christie."

What a life my brother leads! Would my parents let me cruise around all day in the city and go to the Hard Rock with a boy I liked or even with a girl? No, they wouldn't. Now, after being out all day, Alex was probably planning something else fun to do with this girl Christie. While I had to stay at home and get into a dweeby dress and eat dinner with my parents.

One thing I have decided is that I am not showing anybody this journal! How can I let my friends know that in

50

my house I'm treated like a baby? Fortunately, my parents are being understanding enough to let me go to Max's party. If I had to come from out of town like Shanon and Palmer, Mom and Dad probably wouldn't have given their permission. But Mom talked to Mrs. Schloss over the telephone and has given her okay. I can hardly wait! Max told me on the phone that her parents had asked a cousin of hers named Rain Blackburn to play the piano. Max said Rain is a great musician and not to be missed! I can also hardly wait to be out of the house for a night, since Max has also invited me to sleep over after the party. The one problem is that my parents are going out that evening also and will not be able to drop me at the Schloss's house. So, naturally, they asked Alex to take me. I certainly hope no one sees Alex when he drops me off! It would be humiliating if Max found out that I couldn't come to her party without my big brother as a baby-sitter!

CHAPTER SEVEN

Amy's Journal

I could kill my brother Alex—if he doesn't kill himself first!
This morning my parents were actually letting me go out,
but because of Alex, I couldn't go. . . .

Alex, Mom, and I were standing outside of our building.
Mom was there because she was waiting for a taxi. She
was on her way to take some pictures of the mayor, of all
people, for a magazine story. I was there because I was
waiting for my cousin Ping, who was going out shopping
with me. For once my mom had given me permission to go
to some stores. Alex was there because he was going to ride
to Jasmine's house on his motorcycle. My mom and I
watched him get on his bike and put on his helmet. My
parents had said that he absolutely had to wear this whenever he was riding. Besides, it's the law. Then Mom started
to wave for a cab, and I stood there shivering while I
waited for my cousin. Alex drove off.

Two seconds later we heard a car screech. I turned and
looked up to the corner by the stoplight, and there was my
brother! He'd almost been hit by a car, and he'd fallen off

of his motorcycle. I yelled and started running. My mom dropped her camera equipment in front of our building and started running, too. Ping, who was just coming to see me at the loft, started to run after us. By the time we got to the corner, Alex was standing up again and so was his motorcycle. He was grinning, so we knew that he wasn't hurt. But Mom noticed right away and so did I that he wasn't wearing his helmet.

"Where's your helmet?" That's the first thing my mom said.

"I kind of, uh, took it off for a while," said Alex. Cars were honking. The car that almost hit Alex was blocking traffic. The driver had gotten out to make sure Alex was all right.

"What happened here?" my mom said, looking straight at the driver. She sounded kind of hysterical. Then she looked at Alex again. "Are you all right?"

"I'm fine," Alex said in a cheerful voice.

The man who was driving the car apologized. "I didn't see him until the last minute," he said. "I put on my brakes hard. I think I scared him. Sorry."

"You should be sorry," said my mother with her voice rising.

She turned to Alex and glared, then she glared at the helmet. He still didn't have it on his head. He was holding it.

Alex smiled again at the driver. "No harm done, really," he said.

My mother obviously didn't agree. She scowled at the man. "You could have had a serious accident!" she said. "You should concentrate on your driving!"

"Don't worry about it, lady," the driver said. He sounded kind of rude. "Your son says he's all right. Anyway, tell him to wear his helmet!"

"Don't worry," said my mother. "I will!"

The driver got into his car. My mother made Alex drive home again. She watched while he put on his helmet. Ping and I walked back to our building with my mother.

"Everybody upstairs," my mom ordered. "Ping, you're welcome to visit, but Alex and Amy are staying at home today."

"Aww, Ma—" said Alex.

"You weren't wearing your helmet," my mother said sternly. "That was one of the conditions of your having a motorcycle. I haven't got time to deal with this. I have to go to work."

She picked up her camera equipment. (Our superintendent had been watching it while my mom raced up the street to see Alex's accident.)

"I wasn't hurt," Alex grumbled, brushing off his new motorcycle jacket.

"I don't see why *I* have to stay inside," I butted in. "I wasn't almost in a motorcycle accident, and you said Ping and I could go out!"

My mom looked flustered. "I have to go to work," she said. "I'm supposed to be taking pictures of the mayor. I can't worry about what's going on with you kids. I'm too nervous. Please go inside! We'll talk about it later." Then she got a cab and rode away.

I was really angry. It just wasn't fair! Alex did something wrong, and I was being punished.

"I don't really feel like hanging around inside today," Ping told me.

I glared at my cousin. She was only eleven and she was probably going to go somewhere great on her own.

"I know ten-year-olds who go shopping by themselves," Ping muttered.

"This is what I'm up against," I said in a frustrated voice.

Ping went home and I went upstairs. Alex had already gone up before me and was in his bedroom with the door shut. I knocked on it really loud.

My brother opened the door. Of all things, he was smiling. "Close call," he said. "Good thing that guy in the car wasn't going too fast."

"You ought to have your motorcycle taken away from you!" I yelled.

Alex looked puzzled. "What's your problem?"

"That was a stupid thing to do!" I told him. "And because of you, I'm in jail again!"

"It's not my fault if Mom and Dad are protective of you," Alex told me. "You're a girl."

"That's the dumbest thing you've ever said in your whole life!" I yelled at my brother. It was really my parents I wanted to be yelling at, but I couldn't. So I was yelling at him.

"Look, I don't mean to put you down," Alex said, "but it's a crazy city out there."

"Mom grounded me because of what you did!" I exclaimed. "Can't you even say that you're sorry?"

"How can I be sorry for something Mom did?" said Alex.

"Nobody in this house understands me," I said, pacing the room, feeling angry. "You act wild and crazy and because of that I can't do anything and have to act like a total goody-goody."

"Don't blame me for how you act," Alex said. "Chill out, why don't you? I have to call Jasmine and tell her I can't make it."

He gave me a little push to the door, which really irritated me. Then I slammed his door really hard and went to my room. As far as I was concerned, I couldn't care less if I ever talked to my brother again!

That afternoon, my mom came back from her interview. She knocked on the door of my room. "How are you feeling?" she asked.

"Rotten," I said. It was time to tell the truth about how I was feeling for once!

"What did you do this morning?" she asked.

"Nothing," I answered. "Played the guitar."

"Why don't you go to the movies?" she asked.

"With Alex?" I said, absolutely sure that this was the only condition on which I could go.

"Why not?" she replied.

"No thanks," I muttered. I did want to go to the movies, but not with my brother.

"Where would you like to go?" Mom asked. I looked at her. Her face was very apologetic. "I was wrong to say you couldn't go shopping with Ping. I was so upset by Alex's accident, I took it out on you."

"Humph," I said quietly. Well, at least she admitted she was wrong.

"I'd like to make it up to you," she said.

"Then let me get my ears pierced!" I said quickly. "I know a place in the East Village that does it almost for free! Please!"

"We've been through this," my mother said patiently. "Your dad and I don't want you mutilating your ears!"

"But it's not," I whined. "You said you wanted to make it up to me, Mom," I reminded her.

She chuckled. "How about going shopping instead?"

"Okay!" I said, jumping on it. "Can I get what *I* want?"

"What do you have in mind?" Mom asked suspiciously.

56

"Just some regular clothes," I said, trying to be diplomatic. "The clothes I have in my closet are kind of dressy."

My mom lifted her eyebrows. "Don't get anything too wild and crazy," she said. "You know your father . . ."

"I promise," I said, crossing my fingers behind my back.

Just then Alex poked his head into my room. "Hi, Mom," he said with a charming smile. "I heard your voice. Okay if I go out for a while?"

"Sure," Mom said brightly, "you can take Amy shopping."

"I had something else in mind," Alex said. "I was going to meet Christie."

"You can go out with her another time," Mom said matter-of-factly. "Your sister wants to go to the East Village, and I think you owe her one."

Alex sighed and then smiled at me. I didn't smile back, because I was still mad at him.

"Okay, I'll zip Amy down on my bike," he said.

"And don't forget your helmet," Mom said sternly. "Make sure Amy has one on also. And you'd better be extra careful!"

"Yes, Mom," Alex said seriously. He turned and tweaked my hair. "I was thinking of going to the East Village myself. I need a really good haircut."

"A normal haircut, please," my mom warned.

Alex gave Mom a devilish smile. "Of course, Mother," he said. "Don't I do everything the normal way?"

When Mom left my room, I couldn't help giggling. I grabbed the old motorcycle jacket that Alex had given me and put on my new black leather knapsack. Then I met my brother at the front door. He had two helmets, one for each of us.

"Still mad at me?" he said when we were coming down in the elevator.

"Yes," I said. "Because of you I had a boring morning."

"Stick with me, kid," Alex said, putting an arm on my shoulder. "I'll make it up to you."

"Hmm," I said as we walked onto the street. "Those are just the words that Mom used, but she still wouldn't let me get my ears pierced."

"Let's go!" Alex said, jamming on his helmet.

My brother and I sped across town. It was very cold out, but that didn't matter to me. At least I was free! And it was the first time Alex had let me ride on his motorcycle! The first stop we made was my favorite record store, where I found an old Grateful Dead album. Then Alex took me to a thrift store that one of his girlfriends had told him about. I spent half an hour trying on clothes! Alex waited around and gave me his opinion on things. There was a black velvet cape that I liked and an old bowler hat. Also I tried on a black evening dress with sequins but it just wasn't me. Finally, in the bottom of a box, I found a black leather vest with studs that fit me perfectly.

"Buy it, sis," my brother said. "It's you!"

I grinned. It was hard to be mad at my brother anymore, I was having so much fun.

"Dad will think it's awful," I said.

"Wear it at school," Alex advised. "Your friends will appreciate it."

I paid for the vest. It cost twenty dollars! But I think it was worth every penny. That vest made me feel so incredibly cool, especially underneath the old jacket that Alex had given me.

"Okay, my turn," Alex said. We hopped on the cycle again for a brief ride and stopped at a barbershop on Astor Place.

"You're not really going to get a haircut?" I said. "It will take too much time."

"Who cares about the time?" Alex said casually. "Why don't you get one too while you're waiting?"

I considered it, but I really like having long hair now. Inside the barbershop there were a couple of vacant chairs. The haircuts the customers were getting were really wild. One boy was getting his head shaved except for one long rat tail. And a girl had purple and green streaks put in her hair. She actually looked pretty good. Alex sat down in front of a woman barber. The woman, who was young, had on a purple miniskirt, and one side of her hair was purple, too!

"What'll it be?" she asked.

Alex winked at me. "Aren't you going to get your hair cut?" he asked.

I hesitated. There was a man barber with a vacant chair in front of him. "I'll get a trim," I said, hopping into the chair. There was a radio station on in the barbershop that played great oldies. I could see Alex getting his hair cut across the room. The woman barber with purple seemed to be cutting a lot of my brother's hair.

"What kind of haircut are you getting?" I asked Alex over the music.

"Mohawk!" he called to me.

A mohawk? I thought. *What were my parents going to say when they saw that?!*

Alex looked incredible with his mohawk haircut. All that was left of his hair was a very thick wedge in the middle. The sides were shaved clean. "I wouldn't want to be in your shoes," I told him. "You're going to be in trouble."

Alex grinned. "I'm always in trouble. Let's go to the jewelry store."

We zipped off on the cycle again. The jewelry store was a few blocks away. It was the one where I had hoped to have my ears pierced. The jewelry in the window was so original—necklaces and bracelets made out of beads and safety pins and huge earrings that looked very heavy, but turned out to be really light. Once we were in the store the earrings were the first things I looked at. I especially liked a silver pair with lots of hoops.

"Why don't you buy them?" asked Alex.

"They're for pierced ears," I said.

"There's another very similar pair for ears that aren't pierced," offered the saleswoman, overhearing us.

I thought for a moment. I really wanted those earrings. I also really wanted them dangling from real holes in my ears.

"What do you think would happen if I got my ears pierced?" I asked Alex.

"You'd get in trouble," he answered.

"What do you think Mom and Dad would do to me?" I asked.

"Probably ground you," said Alex. "That's what they do to me. But it never lasts too long."

"I'd better not do it," I decided. "Tomorrow is Max's party." There was no way I wanted to miss that!

"Buy the ones that aren't for pierced," Alex offered, trying to be helpful.

That's what I did. I felt like a coward, though. None of my friends would have believed I was such a chicken. I knew that Alex would have pierced his ears whether my parents liked it or not. It was nice of my brother not to rub it in that I hadn't.

"You look great in those, sis," he said when I put on the earrings.

After the jewelry store we went to an Italian café and had these unbelievable pastries. It was then I noticed how

60

dark it was outside. "It must be late," I said in a shaky voice. "We've missed dinner."

"Don't worry," Alex said boldly. "We'll be home in a sec."

Alex was right. We were home in no time. When we took the elevator up to our door, the housekeeper was leaving. Seeing Alex's haircut, she screamed.

"I didn't mean to scare you," Alex apologized.

My mother and father appeared almost immediately. Though my parents didn't scream, they looked just as shocked as the housekeeper.

"Wh-where were you?" my mother managed to get out.

"What's going on with your head?" my father demanded of Alex. Then he caught sight of my new vest. "And what's that thing you're wearing with that beat-up old jacket? It looks like it has nails in it!"

"And your ears!" my mother exclaimed. "Amy, I hope you haven't—"

"Don't worry, Mom," I assured her. "I didn't. I just have new earrings."

My father was pacing. Alex looked nervous. My mom was shaking her head. Oh no! I thought, *they're going to ground me after all, and I didn't even do anything. It's going to be just like always—Alex got a mohawk so I'm going to get in trouble and have to miss Max's party!*

"We were very worried," my dad said sternly, "thinking of Alex on that cycle of his. By the way, your mom told me how you left this morning without your helmet," he added, wagging a finger. "We will discuss your punishment after dinner. And now, Amy—in these strange clothes," he added with a groan. "What are we going to do with them, Pauline?"

"I don't know," sighed my mother. A little smile crept

61

across her face as she looked at Alex and me. "I have an idea," she said. "A special kind of torture."

My father looked shocked for a moment. He watched my mother run to the closet and get her camera.

She began snapping photographs. "Get in the picture, Henry," she said, waving my dad over.

My dad chuckled and Alex and I laughed. My mom was snapping away. Then she set a self-timer on the camera so that she could take a picture of all four of us with herself in it, too!

"This will be our family photograph for the holidays," my father announced. "Alex with his crazy haircut and Amy in her wild clothing."

"And the parents trying to look very cheerful," my mother said, jumping into her place.

My mom and dad stood on either side of us. The camera clicked. My brother and I both smiled.

CHAPTER EIGHT

Vacation Journal—Shanon Davis

Remember what I wrote before about my family being totally normal—I take it back! I hadn't been home for two days when things started getting extremely complicated. My dad, who had been painting my room, and hadn't finished yet, got a bad cold and became a total grouch. My little brothers got chicken pox. My grandmother, Nana, who is getting absentminded, accidentally locked me in the church after Christmas caroling practice. Then she managed to lock herself out of the car. My mom was a nervous wreck about last-minute Christmas shopping. But the worst thing of all had to do with my sister. Poor Doreen! She doesn't want to go back to college, and she picked this crazy time just before Christmas to tell my parents.

My parents were so mad when she told them! First of all, Doreen has already disappointed them. Instead of going to a four-year college like my parents wanted her to, she ended up going to a two-year junior college. And now she wants to drop out of that! Neither Mommy or Daddy went to college at all. In fact, Doreen was the very first Davis to be getting a higher education. My parents were so proud of her when she got into two schools.

Doreen, on the other hand, was not that excited about going. She was glad to be leaving home for a while and meeting new people, but she told me before she left last fall that she was afraid college would be too hard. My sister, even though she's smart, has never liked studying. Unlike me, she's just not into school. She's always liked sports, and in high school she was on the basketball team. She's also a good dancer and she likes having a good time and going out. When Doreen was my age, she had so many boyfriends. I don't even have one—unless you count Mars. This is probably because Doreen is not as shy as I am. It also might have something to do with how incredibly beautiful my sister is.

But no matter how beautiful she is, my dad is furious with her. Last night they had a horrible fight downstairs in the living room. My brothers were upstairs with my grandmother. My mom was wrapping Christmas presents and I was just coming in from walking the dogs.

Doreen was sitting on the piano bench, facing my father. Daddy, who still had his cold, was blowing his nose and pacing.

"Just what do you plan to do if you drop out of school?" Dad demanded, putting his handkerchief away.

"I'll get a job," said Doreen, jutting her chin out. My sister really has a stubborn streak!

"What kind of job?" Dad asked, throwing his hands up.

"I told you," Doreen said. "I'm going to work in a store."

"Doing what?" Dad said with his voice rising.

"Let's try to keep calm, Brad," warned my mother. "Losing our tempers isn't going to accomplish anything."

"I'll lose my temper if I want to!" my dad said.

Oh, no, I thought, *a fight!* There's nothing I hate more than fighting. I hung my parka up on a peg by the door and snuck into the dining area where I could listen. Even though I hate arguing, I had to know what was going on.

"I hate that school, Dad," Doreen said firmly. "You're never going to make me go back!"

"What a wasted opportunity, dear," my mother said softly.

"Wasted opportunity!" yelled my dad. "What about the wasted money?"

"There are more important things than money!" Doreen cried. "I'm not happy at that school."

"Maybe we should think about a transfer," my mother suggested.

"I don't want to transfer," Doreen said, standing up and crossing her arms in front of her. "I don't want to go back to school at all."

"We'll see about this, young lady," Daddy said. "I didn't raise you to be a dumbbell, you know!"

"I'm not a dumbbell!" Doreen said, bursting into tears.

"Well, you're acting like one!" Daddy shouted. "Why can't you be interested in learning? Why can't you make something of yourself? Why can't you be a good student, like Shanon?"

"Let's not compare our girls, Brad," Mommy warned. "Each of them is special in her own way."

Not that again! I thought. My father always compares us! According to Dad, I was the smart one in the family, and Doreen was the pretty one. Doreen must have felt really horrible when Dad practically called her a dumbbell! I know I always feel rotten when he said things like "Doreen was the first in line when they were handing out the good looks!"

65

I peeked back into the living room. My dad was having a sneezing fit, and Doreen was still crying. My mother had stopped wrapping the presents and was trying to comfort her. Nana came downstairs and interrupted everything by tripping on the carpet.

"Watch it, Mom," my mother cried, running over to my grandmother.

"I'm fine," Nana said crisply. "What I want to know is why Doreen is in this state? The boys are trying to sleep upstairs. It's bad enough that they're itching with the chicken pox."

"Your granddaughter wants to work in a store instead of going back to college," my dad announced, throwing his hands up.

"*You* work in a store," Doreen blurted out.

"I am a mechanic," Daddy declared firmly. "I have my own garage. I happen to own a convenience store next to the garage. Yes, sometimes I work in that store. But I own it! You'll never own anything if you don't go to college!"

"That's not true!" cried Doreen. "You didn't go to college and look at you!"

The dogs began to bark. Nana clucked her tongue. My mother pressed her temples as if she had a headache. Doreen tossed her blond curls and flew up the stairs.

"What am I going to do with that girl?" my father groaned in a frustrated voice.

I crept past my parents and grandmother, and I went upstairs to our room.

"Go away," said Doreen.

"What?" I said in surprise.

My sister had angry tears in her eyes. "I need privacy," she insisted. "Go away."

"But this is my room, too," I said. The fact that she was throwing me out hurt my feelings.

"Don't you understand that I'm going through something?" Doreen said impatiently. "Please—I have to think. Why don't you go read a book?"

I gulped and closed the door. I sat at the top of the stairs with my dogs. Why was Doreen mad at me? What had *I* done?

This morning I brought up the subject of going to Max's party again. I had already mentioned it to both of my parents, and they said they would look into it. Mom and I were sitting at the breakfast table. My dad, Doreen, and Nana had already eaten and my brothers were in the living room, watching *Sesame Street*.

"You're going to let me go to my roommate's house in New York, aren't you?" I asked my mother. She and my dad had had enough time to "look into" things.

"It's very expensive just for a weekend," my mom said gently.

"You're not saying I can't go?" I exclaimed.

"We'd like to give you the trip," Mommy said, "but with Christmas . . . there are so many expenses now, Shanon."

"The train fare will only cost around seventy-five dollars," I said with my voice faltering. Of course I knew that seventy-five dollars was a lot of money for my family. But it hadn't occurred to me that they wouldn't be able to come up with it—I wanted to go to the party so badly.

"I'm sorry, dear," my mom said. "You're going to have to say no to this one."

I felt sick. Max had talked so much about her house in New York and the big party we were all invited to. It just wasn't fair. Palmer would definitely be able to go, because her family had lots of money, and Amy of course lived in New York. I thought about Lisa—it had been so long since

I'd seen my best friend. Max had also invited her to the party, and now I would miss seeing her! I crossed my fingers behind my back and made a wish—maybe someone would give me some money for Christmas! Somehow, I had to make it to New York.

Things went from bad to worse today. I was already disappointed and really shocked that my parents weren't going to let me go to Max's. But there was more bad news on the way. . . .

Dad had finally finished the ceiling and trim in the room my sister and I share. It was a beautiful pink color, my favorite. I had gone out to the drugstore in town with Nana to buy some oatmeal bath for my brothers' chicken pox. When we got back it was just around lunchtime. My brothers were sitting in the kitchen eating peanut butter sandwiches and looking very uncomfortable.

"Where's everybody?" I asked Ben.

"Upstairs fixing up Doreen's new bedroom," he said.

I found this statement puzzling. Leaving Nana downstairs in the kitchen, I went up the back stairs. There in the hallway were Doreen, Daddy, and Mommy pushing *my* bed out of *my* room!

"What are you doing?" I asked.

Doreen looked very cheerful. "I'm staying home after the holiday," she announced. "I'm going to find a job somewhere! Isn't it great?"

"Hopefully, it's a temporary arrangement," my dad said.

My mother smiled at me. She looked relieved. "Your sister and father and I had a big powwow while you were out with Nana," she said. "Doreen is going to live at home for the semester."

"But what are you doing with my bed?" I asked. Doreen was pushing it down the hall and Dad was helping her.

"We're giving you your own room," Mom said brightly.

"It's all settled, Shanon," Doreen said over her shoulder. "You're going to have your own room, and so am I. Won't it be nice after all these years to have some privacy?"

I followed them down the hall. Mom was walking beside me. Doreen and Dad were trying to fit my bed into Nana's small sewing room.

"You want me to sleep in there?" I demanded in shock.

"It's small," Mom said with a sheepish expression, "but we thought since Doreen was going to be living at home and you're in boarding school . . ." She looked at me closely. "Don't you like the idea?"

"No, I don't." I was really angry. "I mean you could have asked me! Doreen and I have always shared a room."

Doreen came out of the sewing room. "Come and see, Shanon," she called. "It's a perfect fit!"

I stood at the door of the little room. Dad had painted it a fresh light green color. "I don't like green," I said. "I like pink. How come Doreen gets to have our room?"

"We didn't think you'd mind," my father said, scratching his head. "Of course, Nana's sewing machine will come out."

I peered into the small space. "What about my bookshelf?" I grumbled.

"Oh, we'll move that in," said Dad.

"I want to get things straightened out before Christmas," Mom said, bustling away. "I'm going downstairs to see about the boys. Then I've got inventory to do at the store."

"I have that big Buick to finish working on in the garage," my dad added. "Pack your books up, sweetie pie," he said, giving me a rub on the head. "Later on I'll move in your bookshelf."

69

Just like that, my parents went downstairs. Doreen hurried back down the hallway. "Look how much more space I've got," she said, looking into *our* room.

"This is totally unfair," I muttered. I hate fights, but I had to say something.

"Gee," said Doreen, "I really didn't think you'd mind. You're hardly ever home. I guess I should have told you first. Sorry."

"Just because I go to boarding school doesn't mean that I don't want to have a room at home," I said. "I live here, too, you know."

"Please don't make problems," my sister pleaded. "I just now worked things out with Mom and Dad. They're letting me stay home for a semester."

"Great," I said, "but I don't see why I have to get kicked out of my room because of that."

Doreen took my hand. "Don't you think that thirteen years is long enough for us to share the same room?"

I felt like crying, but I wasn't going to let her see that. I wouldn't have minded sharing a room with my sister forever. But that's not what I said to her. "I suppose if I really think about it, thirteen years in the same room with you *is* enough!" I blurted out angrily.

"You could try to be understanding," she said.

"Okay," I said, "why don't you go live in the sewing room?"

"Because I need the space," she sputtered, "and because I'm the oldest, and it was my room first!"

I was furious. But I didn't say anything. I'm such a coward when it comes to fights.

"I hope you're very happy in *my* room!" was all I could say.

*   *   *

Actually my new room isn't that bad. Doreen was

70

right—my things do fit perfectly. Though I'm still angry about being kicked out of my real room, it's been hard to think about it with Christmas coming up so soon. Another thing that distracted me was getting my first period. Mommy was out at the time, but Doreen and Nana were here, and they were very nice to me. I've been waiting for a long time to get it. It's exciting that the time has come.

Doreen has been very nice to me. I think she might be trying to make up for kicking me out of my room. She even offered to let me sleep in my own room for the rest of the vacation. I said no. It's been fun arranging my things in my new room just the way I want them. Fortunately, it's also been peaceful around here. My brothers are almost over their chicken pox, and my parents are less nervous and grouchy.

I got a letter from Mars in today's mail! It came with a long skinny box, which says, "Do Not Open Until Christmas." I can hardly wait to see what's inside it. As always, my pen pal's letter made me smile.

Dear Minerva, (this is your new name!)

The first thing that happened when I got home was that my mom made me clean out my room and then go up to the attic. The present I am sending you for Christmas is something I found there. I wish I could see you again soon. Hope you are not insulted that I'm calling you Minerva. Of all the goddesses, she is the smartest. Since you are a brain, I thought that was a good name for you.

> *Yours coolly,*
> *Mars (the name of a god, too!)*

The only thing that I didn't like about Mars's letter is the fact that he called me a "brain." Doesn't anyone think of me as anything but smart? I would prefer it if Mars thought of me as pretty, but of course Dad is right—Doreen was first in line for good looks.

My sister and I did some last-minute shopping today. I had already bought most of my presents: a pin in the shape of a flower for my mom, a fishing cap for my dad, a huge hair clip for Doreen, a video game and some trucks for my brothers, and a fancy pincushion for Nana. Tomorrow I'll go Christmas caroling and make cookies with Nana. We already put up our tree. I love Christmas!

If only I could go to Max's party.

CHAPTER NINE

Shanon Davis's Journal

For Christmas I got:
  A pink blouse and navy blue skirt made by Nana
  A New Kids on the Block T-shirt from Doreen
  A dictionary from my aunt Tess
  A new pair of ice skates
  A telephone book with a cloth cover from my mother
  Some barrettes and stickers (smile) from my brothers
  Twenty dollars from my father!
  Lipstick, perfume, and stockings from the whole family.
  From Mars, a dozen red silk roses that used to belong to his mother. Isn't that romantic! These were no ordinary, everyday plastic flowers. When I opened the box, my dad teased me and said, "Got a boyfriend, huh?" I wish!
  Christmas morning was wonderful!
  Christmas afternoon, I had a fight with Doreen. A real one. I guess it had been coming for a long time.
  We'd already been to church and had a big breakfast. My brothers were downstairs playing with their toys, and

Mom and Dad were clearing up the wrapping paper and mess around the tree. My sister had disappeared upstairs a little while earlier. Though things have been better between her and my parents, Doreen didn't seem as happy as she usually is on Christmas. I went into "our" room. She was stretched out on the bed with a lot of newspapers.

"Haven't you ever heard of knocking?" she said crossly.

Oh, brother! I thought. *She's in a bad mood again and on Christmas!*

"I'm not used to knocking," I said. "This used to be my room—remember? I came to try on the skirt and blouse Nana made for me."

My sister let out a sigh and buried her head in one of the newspapers.

"You certainly are grumpy for Christmas," I muttered.

Doreen sat up suddenly and slammed the newspaper on the floor. "When you're my age, maybe you'll have something to be grumpy about, too!" she snapped.

"Give me a break," I said, stepping into my new skirt. "I didn't mean to bother you. I just came in here out of habit."

"Well, you are bothering me," Doreen said angrily. "Everybody in this family is bothering me!" she added, looking as if she would cry.

I took a big breath. "Thanks a lot!" I said. "Have I complained about your kicking me out of my room? Have I accused you of practically ruining everybody's holiday with your problems?"

Doreen gasped. She has a hot temper. Not only that, I think she was surprised that I had stood up to her. "I haven't ruined everyone's holidays," she sputtered. "The only person who's had a bad holiday is me! First, Mom and Dad give me a hard time because I don't want to go

74

back to a school that I hate. Then, they force me into getting a job!"

My sister looked helpless and frustrated. I was confused.

"I thought you wanted a job," I said.

"I do," exclaimed Doreen, "but not just any job. Oh, I don't know what I'm going to do!" she said, tossing the rest of the newspapers down.

"Oh, I get it," I said, sizing up the situation. "You told Mom and Dad you wanted to stay at home and work, and they said you could as long as you got a job, but now you can't find one—right?"

"How can I find a job, living in such a small town?" Doreen said, walking around the room. "All I want is a silly store job, until I find out what I really want to do."

"Maybe it's silly to want to work in a store in the first place," I suggested. I was trying to be helpful.

"You would say something like that," Doreen said with a glare. "You're such a goody-goody. You'll probably go to college just like Mom and Dad want me to do. You'll probably bring home all A's just like always! Who knows what will happen to me?"

Something inside me started boiling. My sister was acting as if she was the only one in the whole world with feelings! "Just who are you calling a goody-goody?" I said, raising my voice. I slammed the door to the room. This was going to be a real fight and I didn't want anyone hearing us.

"Well, aren't you?" Doreen said, her eyes burning into mine.

"Just because I like to study doesn't mean I'm a goody-goody," I screamed. "And just because you hate your school doesn't mean that other people in this house don't have a right to be happy!"

75

"I haven't made anybody unhappy!" Doreen yelled.

"Yes, you have!" I cried. "You made Mom and Dad unhappy and you made me unhappy because you took my room away from me!"

"Take your old room, if you want it so much!" said Doreen. "What difference does privacy make if the rest of your life is horrible? Someday you'll know what it's like to grow up."

"I hope I don't feel sorry for myself the way you do," I told her.

"You're really making me angry," my sister said threateningly. "I have a problem. I don't like school. And you're belittling it."

"No, I'm not," I said. "You're blowing your problem up! You're making it the biggest problem in the world! You wanted to stay home from school, and Mom and Dad let you. Now you're blaming everybody because you can't find a job. Dad's right. You don't really want to make anything of yourself. Not only that, I'd rather be a goody-goody than a dumbbell!"

As soon as the word "dumbbell" came out of my mouth, I wished I could take it back. My sister got quiet, and she looked so hurt! I really don't think of my sister as a dumbbell! I think that she's great. The only reason I called her that was that I was angry, and I'd heard Dad say it when he was angry. "Hey, listen, I'm sorr—" I mumbled. I was trying to get out an apology, but before I could even finish Doreen threw a pillow at my head.

"Goody-goody," she said. "All you do is try to impress Mom and Dad with how smart you are!"

"I want them to be proud of me," I yelled. "Is that a crime?"

"Of course not!" Doreen said. "It's just that . . . you're

lucky that you have something that they can be proud of! You're lucky . . . you're smart!"

She threw herself on the bed and started crying and crying. I felt so bad for Doreen that I wanted to cry, too. My mom knocked on the door all of a sudden.

"What's going on in there?" she said, opening the door a crack.

"It's okay, Ma," Doreen wailed into her pillow.

"We're all right," I gulped, facing my mother.

"I hope the two of you aren't fighting on Christmas," my mother scolded. "I'm surprised at you, Shanon," she said. "Now you two apologize to each other." Then without waiting to see if we did, she shut the door behind her.

I stood with my back pressed against the door. Doreen was still sobbing but not as loudly.

"You're not a dumbbell," I said. "I'm sorry."

Doreen lifted her head up. "And you're not a goody-goody," she sniffed. "You're right. I've been taking my problem out on you."

We looked at each other. Doreen's eyes were puffy. But I still thought she looked pretty. "Maybe you should work in television, instead of a store," I suggested. "Who cares how smart you are? I'm sure you're pretty enough."

Doreen smiled a little. "That is NOT what I need to hear, Shanon," she said.

"You know what I mean," I muttered. "Not very many people in the world look like you."

"Thanks," said Doreen, wiping her eyes.

"You're also smart," I volunteered.

"Sure," said Doreen. "Oh, I know I'm not an actual moron, but the college life is just not for me. I've tried to tell Mom and Dad that but they never listen."

I picked up the newspaper. "Maybe if you didn't want to

77

work in a store," I said, "maybe if you wanted to do something more ambitious . . ."

"Like what?" said Doreen.

"Maybe work in an office," I suggested. "Be a secretary."

"I suppose I could try," said my sister. "The problem is that Brighton is such a small town, there probably aren't too many office jobs." She kicked at the newspaper. "There aren't any openings for store clerks, that I can tell you."

I sat down next to her on the bed. "What is it you want to do actually?" I asked.

"I'm not sure," Doreen said helplessly. "I just don't want to go back to school."

"Well, at least you've got that much," I said.

"Yes, I'm home for a semester," she sighed. "That should give me time to figure my life out, even if I don't manage to get a job. Anyway, I've got some money saved."

"You don't need much money at home living with your parents," I said, looking on the bright side.

"Someday I'd like to move away from Brighton," Doreen said with a far-off look in her eyes. "I'd like to go to New York to live."

"I want to go to New York, too," I said sadly. "Only I don't want to live there. I just want to go to Max's party."

Doreen gave me a sympathetic look. "Too bad Mom and Dad won't let you go," she said. "Was it only because of the money?"

I nodded. "Even with the twenty dollars Daddy gave me for Christmas, I haven't got enough."

My sister looked thoughtful. She got up and brushed her hair at the mirror. "Why don't I give it to you?" she said.

"Give me what?" I asked.

Doreen shrugged and smiled. "The rest of the money you need for your trip," she said. "How much is it?"

"Around fifty-five dollars," I said.

"I can give you that much," said Doreen.

My mouth dropped open. "I couldn't take it. You don't have a job."

"Like you said, I'm living at home," said Doreen. "I have a lot of savings left from when I worked the gas pump this summer."

My heart started to pound. "Are you sure you wouldn't mind? It could be a loan."

My sister gave me a peck on the cheek. "How about a gift?" she said. "I know that if the day comes I'm ever in a jam, you'll help me, won't you?"

I smiled at her. "You know I would."

"Then, Merry Christmas," said Doreen.

I was so happy I almost started laughing. I stood beside my sister and looked in the mirror. "I've got a big pimple," I said. "I hope it disappears before I go."

"Who cares?" Doreen said casually. "You're still pretty."

"I am?" I asked.

"Sure you are," she said. "What are you going to wear to the party?"

"I don't know," I exclaimed. "I don't really have anything dressy."

Doreen opened her closet and winked at me. "Let's see what we can cook up. . . ."

I sat on Doreen's bed while she pulled things out of her closet. Over the years she has managed to get some nice clothes. Of course my sister has such a great body, she'd look good in anything. Settling back on the bed while Doreen pulled out her old party dresses, I realized this was one of the best times my sister and I had had the whole vacation. It seemed funny to me, because we'd had a real fight. Maybe when two people have something on their minds they need to discuss, fighting isn't such a bad thing. I had certainly gotten a lot of things off my chest. And now I had the trip to look forward to, thanks to Doreen. I talked to Mom and Dad and they agreed to let me go. Mom called Max's mother. Everything's set!

Here's a letter I got from Mars!

Dear Shanon,

I saved your present until Christmas morning. I liked the homemade Christmas card you made. You really are an old-fashioned girl. I also liked the candy cane on top of my present. My mom and dad were curious about you, and my brother was razzing me. I had a girl pen pal. *Everybody was also ultra-impressed when I opened your present and discovered the magic kit you sent me. Now I will be El Marzo! the great wizard. Seriously, babe, this works right into my plans. Not that I'm planning to be a magician, but I met a man who runs a professional clown school and I'm thinking about clowning. Maybe I can be a clown who does magic tricks, ha, ha! Remember what a great time I had entertaining the kids at Brighton Hospital when I did my school community service unit. What do you think of my idea to be a clown someday? I like to make people laugh. Give me your opinion. When I told my dad I might become a clown, he said nothing. I don't think my family takes me seriously. Does anyone take me seriously? Do you? By the way, are you going to that party in New York at Maxie's? I wish that magic kit you gave me would take me there. I miss you. Never thought there would be a reason I'd want to hurry back to school in New Hampshire. But there is a reason—y.o.u.!*

XXX, Your pen pal, "El Marzo"

This is what I wrote back to Mars.

Dear Mars,

I am glad you like your magic kit. I also think you'd make a great clown! I am going to Max's party! At first I didn't think I'd be able to. I really wish you were invited. Lisa has been invited and I'm hoping to see her. I wish the magic kit I gave you could transport you places. Right now I'd like you to be transported to my room. That way you'd see where I put the beautiful silk roses you sent me. They are such a lovely gift. Thank you. I told my mom I am still writing to you and she says "hi!" My brothers just got over the chicken pox. My grandmother is great. And even though she's been having some problems, my sister is great, too. I miss you, too.

Yours,
Shanon

P.S. I'm glad the roses you gave me are fake. That way they will never die.

CHAPTER TEN

Amy's Journal

Terrible two's, terrible teens
When will they ever be over
I'll take my place
On life's grand stage
Then they'll see, then they'll know
The face, the voice of my soul
I am waiting, waiting
For that moment, for my moment

This is the new verse to my song.

Shanon's Journal

I am really nervous. Thanks to my sister I'm getting to go to Max's party, but I still don't have the right thing to wear. Nana altered one of Doreen's party dresses for me. When Doreen wore it, she looked like a princess. I definitely know that I don't. I look like someone wearing her older sister's dress. Not only that, I got a letter yesterday from Lisa!

Dear Shanon,

I can't meet you in New York at your roommate's party. My dad won't let me. But something else really nice has happened for me! It has to do with Rob. I have to go! I'll write about it in my journal which I will send.

Love,
Lisa

One of the main reasons I was going to New York was to get to see Lisa! And now she's not coming. Amy and Palmer are a whole lot more social than I am, and Max is probably inviting some of her friends from her old school. I can see myself now all alone at the party, surrounded by Max's father's celebrity friends, dressed in a dress that doesn't look good on me. Maybe this wasn't such a good idea.

Palmer's Journal

Dad says he's sad to let me leave early. I'm kind of sad too, but some things are more important—like parties. Anyway, he has Georgette for the rest of the vacation. So now little Miss Perfect will have Frankie and my dad all to herself. I still can't get over how such a cute guy would like my sister. I wonder what kind of boys will be at Max's party? Maybe the sons of famous actors, since Mr. Schloss is a famous actor. Max's parents are also very rich. I wonder if Max's house is as big as mine. It should prove to be an interesting weekend.

Max's Journal

Everything is all set for the party, except that Lisa Mc-Greevy can't come. I got another letter from Jose.

Dear Max,
I think you made a mistake, because there is no Santa Claus. There was hardly any presents for any of us, and we were good.

> *Yours truly,*
> *Jose*

Poor Jose! I guess I made a mistake in telling him that the proof of Santa's existence was in the good things that happen at Christmas. So I sent him this letter right away.

Dear Jose,
When I was a kid like you, sometimes I would get disappointed at my Christmas haul also. But even if we are good, sometimes Santa Claus runs out of things. Also making all that stuff at the North Pole is hard work. Maybe the elves just couldn't hack it anymore. Or maybe they went on a strike. I'm sure you got some of the things you wanted anyway. Try not to be a bad sport. Tell Lila, Becky, and Billy I said "Hi!"

> *Your pen pal,*
> *Maxie*

PART TWO

CHAPTER ELEVEN

"Don't do anything weird tonight, okay, Gary?" Max faced her three younger brothers in the long corridor outside their room. The oldest, Gary, had an impish grin on his face.

"Don't worry, we won't embarrass you," said Gary.

"Not much, you knucklehead!" teased Brian, plucking his brother's head from behind.

"Quit it, you moron," griped Gary. With a big grin he stomped Brian's toe.

"Ouch!" yelled Brian, running after his brother. "I'll get you for that, Bozo!"

Max's youngest brother Kevin started to giggle. "Don't worry, Maxie," he lisped, peeking from behind a potted palm in the hallway. "When your friends come, we won't act like idiots. We'll be serious—honest." Then he joined the fray with the two older boys in their room.

"And remember not to let any of those frogs out of the terrarium either!" Max yelled into their doorway.

The three "monster pip-squeaks" shut the door in her face and began to roar in hysterics. *What was so funny?* Max thought hopelessly. How could anybody get a laugh out of being banged on the head and stomped on the toe?

What was so hilarious about mentioning her brother's frogs and toads? Gary, Brian, and Kevin certainly wouldn't dare let their animals loose while her friends were there, Max assured herself. Certainly not after they'd gotten in trouble for letting their snake play under the Christmas tree.

"What's wrong, honey?" asked Monica Schloss, sailing out of the master bedroom. Max's mother was wearing a white dress with a bold poinsettia print on it. She was also holding a big checklist.

Max grabbed her. "My friends are going to think I live in an insane asylum!" she said dramatically. "I'm worried."

Mrs. Schloss chuckled. "Come now, we're not that bad, are we?"

"The pip-squeaks are," Max groaned.

"I've asked you not to call your brothers that," her mother murmured, looking over her checklist.

"Call them whatever you like," Max said, following her mother down the corridor, "they're embarrassing. All they do is call each other 'knucklehead' and run around giving people nooggies. Why did Dad have to show them those videos of *The Three Stooges* show? Can't anybody in this family be serious?"

"That's the most ridiculous thing I ever hoid," said Mrs. Schloss in her best Groucho Marx voice.

"Not you, Mother!" Max complained loudly. "I thought I could count on you to act normal." Drawing in a sudden breath, Max eyed her mother in horror. "That dress— you're not going to wear it tonight?"

"What's wrong with it?" Mrs. Schloss demanded, smoothing the huge red and green flowers on her full skirt.

"It's weird," Max said breathlessly. "I'd better get hold of myself," she whispered.

"My sentiments exactly," said Mrs. Schloss. She tugged

Max's curls. "I'm sure your friends will like the party," she assured her. "And as for the behavior of the 'pip-squeaks,' rough-housing and acting up *is* normal for eight-, nine-, and ten-year-olds."

Max peeked out from behind her hands. "And your dress?" she asked.

Mrs. Schloss laughed heartily. "If you hate this one, you should see what I'm actually planning to wear—"

"What?" breathed Max, dreading the worst.

"It's bright orange and gold," teased Mrs. Schloss, starting downstairs. "Kind of Hawaiian-looking with turquoise flowers! And with it, I'm wearing some bright red beads and a wreath of flowers in my hair."

Max giggled. "You're kidding, right?"

"Yes, I'm kidding," Mrs. Schloss called out brightly. "Now instead of worrying about us, go help Mrs. Dobbins fix up your room for Shanon, Amy, and Palmer. I've got to run. The people are here to lay the dance floor in the front parlor. And any minute I'm expecting the piano tuner. We don't want your cousin Rain to play on a piano that's out of tune, do we?"

"Of course not," Max said, smiling. All the talk about Shanon, Amy, and Palmer coming and having the piano tuned for Rain had taken her mind off of her mom's weird clothes and her pip-squeak brothers. Besides, no matter how strange her family was, Max knew that deep down they were good people.

"There's some mail for you in the front hall!" her mom yelled after her.

Max lunged for the banister and slid down. She'd help Mrs. Dobbins with her room later. Mail was more important!

Bumping to the bottom of the stairs, Max grabbed an envelope with her name on it from her mother. Monica

Schloss was leafing through late Christmas cards. "Here's a card from the Smiths," she said, sighing. "They're not going to make the party this year. Listen to this, Max," she said with a giggle. " 'We're certainly going to miss Big Max's clowning around. The holidays won't be the same without a visit to your house.' "

"Very nice," Max said uncomfortably. "Dad isn't going to do any clowning around this year, though, right? He's not going to do that Christina Jean Queen imitation or wear a Santa Claus suit—right?"

"Well, he promised he wouldn't," she said with a wink. "Who's your letter from?" she asked curiously.

"My pen pal, Jose," Max replied. She smiled at the childish scrawl on the envelope. "I can tell by his handwriting."

"Well, hurry on back up and help Mrs. Dobbins," Monica Schloss instructed. "I'm going to see what's going on in the front parlor."

Breezing past the row of "Big" Max's antique armor, Monica Schloss went into the parlor. It was the room where Max's cousin Rain Blackburn would play the piano that night. The food and drinks would be served in the living room where the Christmas tree was. A staff of caterers was already in the kitchen fixing fancy food for the adults and mile-long hoagies for the kids. Max sighed. What an exciting day it was! Perching on the bottom of the stairs, she opened her letter.

Dear Maxie,

How much time does it take to make a doll? That's what Becky wanted. It ain't that hard to put ice skates together, I know. But Santa didn't do it for Billy. And there's no books for Lila and me.

All we got was underwear and socks. It was all laid out nice, but we wondered where were the toys. You said Santa

90

Claus was too busy but my mom said that he knew that we needed that stuff under the tree more than toys. I think I believe you, Max. Santa Claus was just too busy. Or maybe he's just not fair.

See you at the liberry sometime when you get back.

Merry Christmas and a Happy New Year.

Jose

Max stared at the letter for a long time. It was sad to think that Jose and his brothers and sisters had such a disappointing Christmas. She looked around her. Her mother had hired an army of people to get ready for the party. There was a piano tuner at the grand piano in the front room, and people laying a dance floor. The caterers were in the kitchen. . . .

"It isn't fair," Max thought wistfully. How is it that her family could have so much and the Hurt family so little? Was it just because her father could tell jokes and make people laugh? Jose's foster dad was a house painter and a farmer. Max was sure he didn't make much money. After the fire in Brighton the summer before, they didn't even have their own home. Mr. and Mrs. Hurt, Jose, and the other children lived in a trailer. Wasn't painting a house for someone and planting and harvesting their food just as important as telling jokes?

Gary, Brian, Kevin, and she had been given so many presents for Hanukkah and Christmas that Max could hardly keep count. Yet Jose and his brother and sisters were disappointed. And they'd asked for so little! And deep down Max knew that it wasn't the fault of Santa Claus. It was just the way the world was.

Why is the world the way it is? Max thought in frustration. If only there were something she could do to change it.

CHAPTER TWELVE

Shanon peered out through the windows of the long gray limousine that Max's parents had sent to pick her up at the train station. In the front seat was the Schloss family's chauffeur Ollie. Shanon had met him when he'd dropped Max off at school. Marveling at the snarl of traffic in the city streets and the fast pace of the crowd on the sidewalks, Shanon craned her neck to see more. New York certainly was exciting. The sidewalks were so crowded, people could barely walk down the street without bumping. And the number of shops and stores was astounding! Decked out in twinkling lights and holiday finery, the store windows looked so beautiful. There were lines of people outside looking at them. She wanted to ask the chauffeur to stop so that she could get out and have a closer look, but she didn't dare. She'd never been to New York, and she'd never been in a limousine either. At the moment, as much fun as it was to view the "Big Apple" for the first time, she found riding by herself in a car that was half a block long rather intimidating. Pressing her back against the plush seat of the enormous car, Shanon shut her eyes for a moment. Inside, her heart was racing. She'd made it! Taking a trip to New York or some other city just for a weekend was probably old hat to Amy, Max, and Palmer. Even Lisa's family, though they weren't exceptionally rich, went on trips together that Shanon's folks could never dream of taking. At Alma Stephens when they were living together in the same suite, it was easy to forget that the girls' backgrounds were so different—that Max and Palmer, especially, came from such wealthy families and that Shanon's parents couldn't afford to send Shanon to Alma Stephens without her scholarship. But now, being driven in the Schloss family car, Shanon was very aware of the difference. She began to feel nervous about meeting Maxie's family—Mr. Schloss was a famous television star! And from what Max had said, there would be a lot of other show business people at the party. Shanon gulped. If only she'd thought to ask for a new dress for Christmas so that she wouldn't have had to wear one of her sister's hand-me-downs. She could only imagine the gorgeous outfits Max and Palmer would be wearing! Palmer would have something in turquoise blue, Shanon guessed with a smile to herself. And Max would probably wear something very bright and stylish. As for Amy . . . Shanon giggled a little out loud . . . what would Amy wear to such a fancy party? Shanon imagined her suitemate arriving at Max's dressed in all black leather. She secretly hoped that Amy *would* wear something outrageous. Maybe then nobody would notice the dress she'd borrowed from Doreen. In Shanon's mind the dress began to seem more and more drab as they entered the Schloss's elegant uptown neighborhood.

The limousine stopped outside of a stately three-story brick house.

"Is this it?" she asked shakily. Ollie had gotten out and

opened her door. He was extending a gloved hand in her direction.

Awkwardly grabbing the chauffeur's hand, Shanon hoisted herself from the car. Ollie reached into the middle seat to get her luggage. Shanon gazed up at the big house, starry-eyed. A three-foot-high pine wreath with a velvet bow hung on the polished wood door, and there was a candle in every window.

Three men carrying white boxes appeared next to Shanon.

"The service door is over there to the left," Ollie directed them. "Those must be the pastries," the chauffeur said to Shanon confidentially. The men marched past Shanon and into a side door. The air was filled with a delicious aroma as they passed. Ollie came up beside Shanon carrying her luggage. "We can go in," he said politely.

Glancing at the toes of her worn brown boots, Shanon nodded nervously. How she wished she'd thought to wear something more dressy on the train. She had on green ski pants, her beret and parka. The Schlosses were probably very formal people, she told herself. They wouldn't expect her to wear pants at their house.

As the chauffeur opened the door, a man's voice boomed from inside. "Is she here?" the voice called. "Good work, Ollie! Take the bags upstairs!"

Shanon stepped inside timidly and was immediately bowled over by the owner of the big voice. Red-haired, zany-eyed Maximillian Schloss had a face known in every home in America. Shanon could hardly believe she was seeing the famous TV comedian face-to-face.

"You've got to be Shanon!" Mr. Schloss exclaimed in delight. Taking both her hands, he pulled her forward. "I'm Max," he said with a big grin. "Since there's two

94

Maxes in the house, you'd better call me Big Max!"

Shanon blushed with shyness and pleasure. She liked Maxie's father right away. "How do you do?" she said, formally.

"How do I do?" he quipped. "I do okay, I guess. Come on in and see the place!"

The "place" was enormous! Shanon thought that the entire first floor of her home in New Hampshire could fit in Max's front hall. She blinked. Every wall was filled with brightly colored paintings. Flowers were everywhere! Her eyes widened as she took in a collection of antique armor.

A woman in a flowered dress and red beads came forward. "Shanon, I'm so glad you came!" she said. "I'm Monica Schloss." She put a friendly arm around Shanon's shoulder. "Maxie!" she yelled. "Your roommate's here! Sorry Maxie couldn't meet you herself," she said. "Her brothers had a little accident, and I asked her to help me."

"That's fine," Shanon murmured.

"Shanon!" Max sang out.

Shanon looked straight up. Her roommate came sliding down the banister!

"Great to see you!" Max cried, jumping off at the bottom. Lunging forward, she gave Shanon a big hug.

"Acch!" Shanon said playfully. "You're squeezing the life out of me!"

Max backed off and giggled. "Sorry, I'm just so glad you're here." Glancing sidelong at her parents, she whispered, "This place is weird, but you'll get used to it!"

"All right, Maxie, don't turn her against us," warned Mr. Schloss humorously. "Besides, tonight I'm going to be cool, calm, and collected. No practical jokes, no . . . nothing." Mr. Schloss put on a serious face. "Of course my friends expect me to act silly, but with your friends here"

95

—he winked at Shanon—"I wouldn't dream of it."

"I'm off to the kitchen," Monica Schloss said, hurrying away. "Glad you made it, Shanon!"

"Thanks," Shanon called back.

"I'm off to the balcony to sneak a cigar," Mr. Schloss whispered mischievously. "Come on," he said, grabbing Shanon. "I'll show you my reindeer."

With a giggle, Shanon let herself be carried off by Big Max while "little" Max brought up the rear. In the rear of a big room with a grand piano were some French doors leading to a small balcony. Through the doors Shanon could see a long sunken garden covered with snow. And in the middle of the yard was a group of fake reindeer!

"Aren't they dopey-looking?" Max said. "My parents are so attached to them."

"Once upon a time you were attached to our reindeer, too," her father said playfully.

"Close the door, Dad," Max griped. "It's getting cold."

Shutting the balcony door behind him, Maximillian Schloss lit up his cigar. From behind the glass he smiled at the girls.

"My dad's really okay," Max said, rolling her eyes.

"I like him," said Shanon.

Max grabbed her hand. "Come on. I'll show you my room."

The two girls ran toward the staircase. "Where did you get those?" Shanon asked, pointing to the collection of armor.

"They're actually petrified Munchkins," Max joked.

Shanon looked at them bewildered.

"My father collects old suits of armor," Max explained, giggling at how serious Shanon looked. She tapped one of the visors. "I used to think there were people in them when he first bought them," she whispered.

The kitchen door flung open and Max's brothers dashed out.

"Hide!" Max warned, leaping onto the stairs.

"Hey, Maxie!" yelled Gary. "Who's your friend?"

"It's Shanon Davis, knucklehead!" Brian answered for her.

"Hi, Shanon!" Kevin lisped with his babyish voice.

Shanon smiled broadly. Max's brothers looked like her—all three of them had curly hair—though unlike Max, the two oldest, Gary and Brian, were blond.

"Speaking of Munchkins," Max said, turning reluctantly, "these are my brothers."

"Better known as the monster pip-squeaks!" Brian announced.

Gary jabbed him with an elbow. "Mind your manners, pea-brain. Don't give Shanon the wrong idea about us."

"It's what Maxie calls us," Brian argued.

Shanon gave Max a look.

"They're crazy," Max whispered. "There's no other explanation. Ever since my dad gave them some *Three Stooges* videos, they've been acting this way. They also fight a lot, so watch out."

"They fight?" Shanon asked softly.

"Pretend fight," Max said with a chuckle. "They roughhouse. Kind of like human Teenage Mutant Ninja Turtles. Oh, and they also play tricks on people. So watch out!"

Shanon smothered a laugh.

"We know you're talking about us, Max," Gary sang out.

"You're a conversation piece," Max teased over her shoulder. "Come on, let's get out of here," she said, grabbing Shanon.

Shanon allowed herself to be ushered to the second floor and down the corridor to Max's big bedroom. Three cots with flowery coverlets were arranged across from Max's bed. Shanon gasped when she saw the tiger mural, and she couldn't believe how terrific the window hangings made of foreign flags looked.

"This is awesome!" she said sincerely.

"I didn't choose the spreads on the cots," Max said critically. "But at least there's enough room for us to all sleep in here."

"You've got a huge bedroom," said Shanon incredulously.

"Sit down," Max said, slamming the door. "I'm glad you're the first one to get here."

"When is everybody else coming?" asked Shanon. She perched on one of the cots.

"Ollie's going to the airport in a while to pick up Palmer," said Max. "Sorry I didn't meet you at the train. My brothers took their frogs for a swim in the guest bathroom and my mother almost had a heart attack. A big party like this is a lot of work, and she's really into it. When she saw what the boys had done, she asked me to stay home and help collect amphibians."

"That's a pretty good excuse," Shanon joked.

"The party should be great," Max continued. "Amy's definitely coming. And my cousin Rain is to die for, he's such a good musician."

"I saw some guys delivering pastries when I came in," Shanon said. "They really smelled yummy."

"There's loads of food," said Max. "My parents invited a lot of people. So don't get shy."

"I won't," Shanon said, blushing.

"I know you by now," Max said, bouncing onto a cot. "You hate a lot of people hanging around. So if you get shy, just go find me, okay?"

"Okay," Shanon promised.

Max jumped up and opened her closet. "Look what I'm wearing!" she announced gaily. At the sight of the amazing red and green plaid taffeta dress with puffy sleeves, Shanon's mouth dropped open. "It's gorgeous," she said. "I knew you'd be wearing something like that."

Max grinned. "Isn't it nice? What are you wearing?" she asked.

Shanon jiggled her foot. "You'll see," she muttered self-consciously.

"Let me see now," Max said, darting toward Shanon's luggage. "You should have your dress hanging up anyway," she added. "Otherwise, it'll get wrinkled."

Shanon got up and reluctantly opened her worn suitcase. Having been packed carefully by Nana, Doreen's old party dress was on top.

Max whistled. "Neat! It's really old-fashioned!"

"Exactly," Shanon muttered, putting the dress down.

"I didn't mean it as an insult," said Max.

"It's one of Doreen's hand-me-downs," Shanon said flatly. "Nana made it for her."

"Wow, a homemade dress," Max said enviously. "I've never had one."

"Thank your lucky stars," Shanon said, gazing down at the dress. When she had tried the dress on at home, all she could think of was how it had looked so much better on her sister. Now that she was at Max's, all she could think of was how dull it was compared to Max's bright red and green one.

"I wish I had something else to wear," Shanon said with a sigh.

"You're welcome to borrow something of mine," Max said generously.

Shanon smiled weakly. "We're not the same size."

Max nodded. "That might be a problem. Anyway—"

she added, picking up Shanon's dress gingerly, "I think this dress looks great. Don't knock it. I bet when you put it on you'll look like Miss America."

"Like Miss Dweeb America," said Shanon.

Max gave her a rough pat on the shoulder. "You'll look great, don't worry about it. Promise me something."

"What's that?" Shanon asked.

"No matter how silly my dad acts or my brothers, you won't hold it against me."

Shanon laughed. "If you don't hold it against me that I'm wearing a dweeby dress to the party."

"Deal!" Max agreed with a grin. "Are you hungry?"

"Starving," Shanon admitted.

"Let's go downstairs and sample the hoagies," Max said gleefully.

"Great," said Shanon, smiling at her roommate. "I've got a lot of stuff to tell you," she said on her way out the door. "Actually, a lot is in my journal."

"I wrote a lot in mine, too," said Max. "But we can look at them later. After we eat I want to show you something else."

"What is it?" Shanon asked.

"Something that's been bothering me," Max admitted. "A letter from Jose. . . ."

CHAPTER THIRTEEN

At six o'clock Palmer arrived at the Schloss house with Ollie. The Schloss's chauffeur made trip after trip to the limousine to retrieve Palmer's luggage.

"How many suitcases did you take with you?" Max asked in amazement.

"I had to bring my California Christmas with me," Palmer replied casually. "Don't forget I'm on my way back to Florida."

"Gosh," said Shanon, watching the bags come through the door, "you must have gotten an awful lot of presents."

"Not as many as my sister," Palmer said promptly. "Besides, lots of the things in my suitcase are just clothes."

"We'll help you with those," Max said to Ollie. "Thanks a lot."

"Very good," said the chauffeur. "I'll just take a few of them up."

Palmer stood in the huge entrance foyer, with the remains of her luggage. On either side of her stood Max and Shanon. "Very nice house," the tall blond said with a tilt of her nose. "It's almost as big as my mom's place in Palm Beach."

"Your house is even bigger than this?" Shanon exclaimed.

Max and Shanon each picked up one of Palmer's duffel bags and started to climb the stairs. "We'd better go up and get ready for the party," Max advised. "My parents are dressing right now. You'll meet them later."

"Wait until you see my dress!" Palmer volunteered, selecting a small makeup case to carry.

Suddenly Palmer was distracted by something—a noise and some kind of movement along the side of the corridor. "What was that?" she said, pointing to the row of diminutive antique armor.

"My dad likes to collect old tin," Max quipped, marching toward the stairway. "Actually, it's armor for midgets."

Shanon followed her, giggling. "In the Middle Ages, people were just shorter, you know that."

Palmer's eyes narrowed suspiciously. She knew that she'd seen someone moving and now she saw it again. A small boy was peeking out from the row of armor doing handstands. Farther down the row there was another small boy's face, sticking his tongue out. And in the farthest corner she could see a small sneaker and hear giggling.

"Come out of there!" Max demanded angrily.

Gary, Brian, and Kevin jumped out and laughed.

"Who are they?" huffed Palmer.

"My brothers," Max said, rolling her eyes.

"How do you do?" Gary said, stepping forward and making a humorous bow.

"How do you do?" Brian followed in imitation.

"We're pip-squeaks," Kevin lisped in explanation. Max's youngest brother gave Palmer a big toothless grin.

Shanon and Max both giggled. But Palmer wasn't amused. "Poor Max," she said. "I only have one small whiner at home to contend with—that's Georgette. To think that you have three!"

"They're okay," Max said protectively. "Better get going to your room, gang," she ordered her brothers. "Mom's going to want to inspect your clothes and you're not even half dressed yet!"

"Okay, Maxie," Gary sang out. Bolting in front of the girls, the three boys took off.

"Did you hear what that blond girl called us?" Gary whispered to Brian on their way up.

"Yeah, a weiner," Kevin volunteered from behind.

"No, a whiner," Gary said over his shoulder.

"How can you stand them?" said Palmer. "All that energy!"

"They're a handful," Max agreed.

"I think they're cute," volunteered Shanon. She nudged Palmer. "Anyway, I thought you liked boys."

"Over three feet tall, please!" Palmer exclaimed. "How many boys have you invited by the way?" she asked Max.

"A couple," Max said hurriedly. She grabbed Palmer's arm. "Want to see the Christmas tree before we go up?"

"Sure," Palmer said, being ushered away. The three girls poked their heads into the living room. The ten-foot-high pine laden with ornaments was breathtaking! Even Palmer was impressed.

"I've never had a tree that big in all my life," she admitted.

"You should see what they've got out back," Shanon exclaimed excitedly. "Reindeer!"

"We'll see those later," Max instructed. "Let's get dressed first. My parents may need me to help at the beginning of the party."

On their way to Max's bedroom, they ran into Mr. and

103

Mrs. Schloss. Monica Schloss was wearing a blue and white silk flowered dress and three strands of big pearls.

"How do you like my dress?" Monica said, giving Max a wink.

Max giggled. "It meets with my approval. This is Palmer Durand," she said, indicating her friend.

"So happy to meet you," Mrs. Schloss said warmly.

"And you must be Maximillian Schloss," Palmer gushed, extending her hand to Max's father. "Before I leave may I have your autograph?"

"Sure thing," said Big Max. "Collect ten of mine and you can trade it for one of Robin Williams's."

Max's parents hurried down the staircase. "When's Rain going to get here?" Max yelled after them.

"Pretty soon I expect! I'll let you know."

"Who's Rain?" Palmer asked, wrinkling her nose. "That's such an odd name."

"He's my cousin," Max explained. "He's a musician."

Palmer sighed as the girls walked into the bedroom. "A musician, huh? How boring."

"But your pen pal Sam is a musician," Shanon pointed out.

"Oh, Sam's not just my pen pal anymore. He's my boy-friend now," Palmer announced nonchalantly. "That's why I don't need to meet another musician. On the plane I was thinking of meeting a football player."

"Your reasoning is beyond me," Max said with a giggle as the girls walked into her room.

"Nice room," Palmer said, stepping over her luggage. "It's almost as big as my room in Palm Beach."

"Is there anything that's as big as yours, Palmer?" Sha-non said.

"What did you say?" Palmer asked.

"Nothing," Shanon replied, sharing a look with Max.

They began to get ready for the party. While Palmer washed up in Max's bathroom, Shanon and Max changed into their clothes.

"Your dress is so beautiful!" Shanon sighed, as billows of red and green taffeta floated down over Max's red head.

"So's yours," Max chirped, smoothing her skirt down.

Carefully removing her homemade, hand-me-down dress from its hanger, Shanon put it on.

"This used to look great on Doreen," she couldn't help saying.

"It looks great on you," Max said, zipping her up. "Remember your promise—don't be shy."

Shanon blushed. Asking her not to be shy at a party was like asking the Empire State Building not to be tall. "I'll try," she promised. "As long as I'm with somebody I know."

Palmer emerged from the bathroom wearing hot curlers. "You'd better hurry up," Max instructed, checking her watch. "Like I said, I have to be downstairs early."

"Go ahead without me," Palmer said generously. "Shanon will wait for me—right?" She smiled at Shanon and Shanon nodded.

"I'll wait for as long as you need me to," she replied. "Maybe we should have our own party up here."

Max threw up her hands. "Do me a favor, Palmer," she said. "Keep an eye on Miss Davis, here—okay?"

"I'll take care of her," Palmer said good-naturedly. She ruffled Shanon's hair. "Stick with the 'pro.' "

"The 'pro'?" Shanon giggled.

"I could call myself that," Palmer said, sashaying to the dresser. "I know how to handle myself at parties." She eyed Max as she put on her mascara. "How many people did your parents let you invite?" she asked.

"Let's see," said Max, counting on her fingers, "there's Juliette, Kathryn, Yvette—they're from my old school. . . ."

"What about the boys?" asked Palmer.

"Oh, Roger and Keith Jeffers," Max said with a shrug. "They were the only boys in my class that I really liked."

"Are they cute?" Palmer asked excitedly.

"It depends on your definition," said Max.

"Well, who else is on the guest list?" Palmer asked, opening a suitcase. "Any television stars?"

"I'm sure some of the cast members from my dad's show will be here," said Max.

"That should be exciting," said Shanon.

"And Faline Trudeau, the owner of the Trudeau Modeling Agency, is coming, too," the tall redhead added.

Palmer lifted an eyebrow. "Faline Trudeau? I've read about her. She's got one of the biggest agencies in New York. Maybe she'll discover me."

Max smothered a giggle. "Be serious."

"I am serious," huffed Palmer. "Lots of fresh young faces are discovered at parties."

"When's Amy going to get here?" Shanon asked, wandering over to the window.

"Soon, I hope," said Max. "She promised she's coming."

Suddenly at the door the girls heard snickering. Max turned sharply and caught sight of the "pip-squeaks."

"We thought you'd like some company!" Gary shouted, throwing something into the room.

Palmer screamed.

"What is it?" Shanon asked, keeping her distance from the dark, squiggly object.

Max laughed. "It's just a rubber snake," she said, walking over to the door. "My brothers' idea of a joke. Make

106

sure you don't go into their room," she warned Palmer. "They've got a real snake in there!"

Standing in her slip, Palmer shivered. "Oh, gross! Gross! There's nothing I hate worse than slimy things."

"Then keep away from my brothers' room," said Max. She looked at her watch, then fluffed her hair at the mirror. "I'm going down," she announced. "My mom gets nervous just before parties. And I'd better make sure my brothers stay out of her hair."

"See you later," Shanon said with a smile.

"See you down there," said Palmer.

Shanon nervously smoothed her hair and put on her new lipstick. She tugged at her hand-me-down dress and tried not to feel self-conscious. But when Palmer pulled a beautiful turquoise velvet dress out of her wardrobe . . .

"That's so pretty," Shanon said with a gulp.

"Yes, I know," Palmer said, snuggling into the dress. "A present from my mom for Christmas."

Afraid that Palmer would see the envious look in her eyes, Shanon turned away.

"Your dress is nice, too," Palmer said, coming up behind her.

"Thanks," Shanon said gratefully.

Palmer spritzed her with perfume. "Come on! Let's party!"

CHAPTER FOURTEEN

Amy and her brother Alex stood next to the Schloss Christmas tree. It was nine P.M. and Maxie's parents' party was in full swing. The huge living room and dining room were filled with loud laughing and chatter. And floating across the corridor from the front parlor were the sounds of a funky ragtime piano. Ordinarily Amy would have made a beeline toward the music, but first she had to settle something with her brother.

"Promise me you won't say anything," she begged, tugging at Alex. "Please . . . for my sake."

"Why in the world did you introduce me to Max as your *date* when we came in?" Alex demanded.

"Because it's embarrassing to have to go everywhere with your brother!" Amy hissed back.

"Look, I don't have to stay the whole time. I just promised Dad I'd make sure you were okay. I don't want to embarrass you," her brother said in an offended tone.

Amy blew out a big breath in frustration. "It's okay. You can stay, but do me a favor—don't blow my cover."

"Okay, sis, oops! I mean, sweetheart," Alex replied with a chuckle. He draped an arm over his sister's shoulder.

"Even though I think you're lucky to be related to a hip dude like me, I will not reveal my identity. But confidentially, I think you're being silly."

"Thanks," Amy said. "I know it seems silly, but remember, I got you in here."

"Am I glad you did," Alex said, his dark eyes lighting on a group of pretty girls near one of the food tables. "Check it out—I'm suddenly hungry."

"Remember, you're my date!" Amy wailed, helpless as her brother waltzed away. She knew better than to expect her independent-minded brother to stick by her when there were pretty girls around.

Amy tingled with excitement as she anticipated a whole evening of freedom. Her mom had even agreed to let her stay overnight! And the party itself looked incredible. There seemed to be hundreds of interesting-looking people, young and old, still streaming in. And whoever was playing the piano in the parlor was sensational! Amy wondered if it could be the cousin Max mentioned over the telephone.

Amy looked around her. Max was busy at another end of the room with some girls from her old school and Amy had lost sight of Shanon and Palmer. As for her "date," Alex, he was already deep in conversation with one of Maxie's prettier girlfriends. Tugging awkwardly at the velvet party dress her parents had insisted on her wearing, Amy giggled softly. Telling Max that Alex was her date *was* kind of silly. But the Foxes were used to thinking of her as totally independent and tough. She didn't want to spoil her image by showing up with her brother.

"Your date seems very friendly," Max gushed, coming up suddenly.

"My, uh, what?" Amy asked, caught off guard.

"Your date with the outrageous haircut," Max said,

pointing across the room at Alex. "You'd better watch out. My old friend Juliette's a boy hunter."

"Uh, that's okay," Amy muttered, feeling a blush on her cheeks. "Alex and I, uh, we're not serious or anything."

"Who cares?" Max said cheerfully. "At least you have a real date! When did you meet him? I can't believe you never told us about him!"

"Speaking of boy hunters," Amy said, changing the subject, "where's Palmer?"

"In here somewhere," Max replied, peering into the crowd. A woman in a silver evening dress brushed past her.

"Hi, Maxie," the woman called over her shoulder, gaily.

"Hi, Faline," Max called back.

"That's Faline Trudeau," Max whispered to Amy. "She's a friend of my mom's. She owns a big modeling agency!"

"Wow," said Amy, watching the woman in the silvery dress enter the crowded room where the music came from.

"I made the mistake of telling Palmer who she was," Max said with a giggle. "You know how Palmer's always talking about how she should be a model, so she's been stalking Faline all night."

Amy chortled. "I thought she'd be checking out the boys!"

"She's doing that, too," Max giggled. "I saw her talking to my old friends Roger and Keith."

"That's my roommate!" said Amy. She tapped her foot and grinned. "I've got to get into the other room," she exclaimed. "The riffs coming out of that piano are truly amazing!"

"Sure thing," said Max, "but don't you want to keep an eye on your date? Palmer might steal him," she teased.

Amy laughed loudly. "Palmer is a preppy all the way. I

110

don't think she'd go for a guy with a mohawk. Besides," she added casually, "Alex can take care of himself."

Max grabbed Amy's hand and steered her through the crowd. The driving rhythm of rock 'n' roll seemed to get the room spinning. "I love your parents' taste in music!" Amy enthused. "Is that your cousin Rain?" she exclaimed, eyeing the handsome guy at the piano.

"Yes!" Max said proudly. "When he's done with this piece, I'll introduce you."

Meanwhile, in the living room, Palmer and Shanon sat wedged together on a small loveseat. They were balancing plates full of food on their laps.

"This is a wild party," Palmer said, gulping her sandwich. "My parents would never think of this—having kids and grown-ups all in the same room. There must be over a hundred people here!"

"Pretty exciting," breathed Shanon, brushing a crumb off her dress.

"Max has so many friends from her old school," commented Palmer. "Not too many cute boys, however," she said critically.

"Don't you like the Jeffers brothers?" Shanon chuckled.

Palmer rolled her blue eyes. "They're too pimply."

Giggling, Shanon felt her own cheek. Fortunately that day her face was unblemished. "Do I look all right?" she asked, nervously touching her hair.

"Great," Palmer murmured, letting her eyes drift.

"Look!" Palmer gasped. "Max's brothers—they're doing something weird at the refreshment table."

"I can't see them," Shanon said, trying to peer through the crowd.

"The little one, Kevin, just took a fistful of black olives," Palmer hissed.

111

"Oh, now I see them," Shanon said, smiling. "Maybe they're getting food for their snake."

"Snakes," Palmer said, making a face. "Yuk! Poor Max, I'd hate to be stuck with three little monsters like that."

"I think they're funny," Shanon said, nibbling a pickle.

"I don't," Palmer huffed, watching the boys leave the room. "I think they're totally undignified."

"Look!" Shanon whispered. "There's Joey Jackson! He's an actor on Mr. Schloss's show!"

"I got his autograph earlier," Palmer informed her. Her eyes opened wide. "Look who's at the refreshment table," she said excitedly. "It's that Faline Trudeau, again. Come on—" she urged Shanon, "let's go! maybe she'll discover us."

"We already stood right next to her just a little while ago," Shanon said, hanging back. "Anyway, I don't want to be discovered."

"Well, I do," Palmer insisted. "Everyone is always saying that I look like a model, aren't they? Sam O'Leary said that even his mother said that about me. And she only saw the picture Sam's got in his wallet!"

"You are the model type," Shanon admitted, "just like my sister Doreen."

"So, let's go," Palmer prodded. "I'm sure that Faline Trudeau has noticed me already. Now all we have to do is meet." Grabbing Shanon by the elbow, she tried to steer her to the food table. "Come on," she hissed. "If you come with me, it will look less conspicuous."

"But I, uh, I don't want to be seen," Shanon balked.

"Don't worry," Palmer said breezily. "She won't be looking at you."

Shanon blinked.

"I'm the one who wants to be a model," the blond added by way of explanation.

112

Palmer eyed Faline Trudeau from across the room. The woman in the beautiful silvery gown was chatting with some other grown-ups in line at the buffet table.

"I'm just going to act natural and be myself," Palmer said, making her way over.

"Sounds great," Shanon said. "Don't do anything embarrassing."

"I'm just going to go over to the buffet table and get something to eat where Faline can see me."

"If you say so," Shanon said, tagging along.

The tall blond teen stepped up to the buffet line with confidence. Shanon followed her sheepishly. Flashing a smile at the man in line behind Ms. Trudeau, Palmer edged in.

"You're breaking in line," Shanon whispered with a blush.

"Nobody cares," Palmer whispered back confidently. She tossed her blond curls and kept smiling.

"What are you smiling at?" Shanon whispered.

"Nothing," Palmer said through clenched teeth.

Suddenly Faline Trudeau turned toward them.

Shanon blushed and Palmer gulped.

"Can I help you fix a plate, Ms. Trudeau?" Palmer asked, recovering herself.

"I don't mind waiting," the woman replied graciously. "Though I must say my mouth is watering for some of that shrimp."

"Shrimp, coming right up!" Palmer exclaimed, leaping out of the line. Shanon watched in embarrassment as her friend crashed in at the front. And her face reddened even more when she felt Faline Trudeau's gaze fall upon *her*.

"What service," the woman said, giving Shanon a playful smile.

"She's worked as a waitress," Shanon muttered, feeling

113

obligated to answer. "Not at a real restaurant but at our school snack bar."

"Are you two school friends of Maxie's?" the woman asked Shanon warmly.

Shanon nodded. "I'm Maxie's roommate."

Palmer arrived with a big plate of shrimp.

"I put some cocktail sauce on the side," she said brightly.

"Thanks a lot," Ms. Trudeau said graciously.

Palmer stood very close and smiled broadly. "My, uh, name is Palmer Durand," she offered.

"Nice meeting you, Palmer," said the woman. She nibbled one of the shrimp and offered the plate to the man standing in front of her. "Compliments of Maxie's school friends," she said with a soft laugh. "They're really cute."

Overhearing the compliment, Palmer smiled in triumph. Then she edged back in line next to Shanon. Faline Trudeau turned back around again.

"And what's your name?" she asked, her eyes again lingering on Shanon.

She looked away self-consciously. "Shanon Davis," she muttered, smoothing her dress.

Now at the front of the line, Faline Trudeau helped herself to more food and then walked away with her companions. Palmer flashed her one last big smile. "Nice meeting you, Ms. Trudeau!" she called out after the owner of the modeling agency.

Shanon stared at the buffet food. "I'm stuffed, too many hoagies," she said.

"Me, too," Palmer agreed, leaving the line.

"You were really nervy," Shanon said as the girls walked toward the Christmas tree. "I could never go up and introduce myself to someone important like the owner of a modeling agency."

"I just hope she noticed me enough," Palmer said.

114

"She definitely noticed you," Shanon assured her friend. "You were right on top of her."

"Good," said Palmer. "Hopefully, she'll think of me the next time she needs a model."

A burst of applause from the other room interrupted them. "Want to go in to hear the music?" asked Shanon. "We haven't even been in there yet."

"Sure," said Palmer. "Maybe there are some cuter boys in there our age."

In the large front parlor, Amy stood by the grand piano, mesmerized by Rain Blackburn. The tall, auburn-haired boy in the wire-rimmed glasses was an extraordinary musician. He was also amazingly good-looking. Rain's chiseled profile furrowed as his hands flew across the keyboard. Amy marveled at his dexterity, the subtlety of his touch, and his incredible gift for musical improvisation. It was hard to put a word to what Rain's style was. Starting off with a simple popular tune, the pianist wove melody after melody, displaying his virtuosity in jazz, ragtime, and rock.

Amy wasn't Rain's only admirer. Adults and teens alike flocked around the piano in awed silence. And the portable dance floor was packed with dancing couples. On the edge of the crowd stood Palmer. Her eyes on Rain Blackburn's handsome profile.

"Who's that boy?" she breathed, clutching Shanon's arm.

"It's Max's cousin," Shanon whispered, trying to hear the music.

Palmer just stared. The young man at the piano had to be the cutest boy she'd ever seen. "I think I'm going to die," she said, fanning herself.

"Stop acting like a jerk," said Shanon.

"I'm serious!" hissed Palmer, staring dreamy-eyed. "I've never felt like this before in my life."

Shanon gave Palmer a sidelong look. After living with her at school, she knew Palmer only too well. "Don't tell me you're having another one of your instant crushes?"

"This time it's a real heart attack," Palmer admitted. She gazed at Rain. "I've got to meet him!"

The crowd around the piano listened excitedly as Rain finished his set. Applause burst from the dance floor along with shouts of approval.

"Nice going, Rain," Max Schloss boomed, appearing from the sidelines, where he'd been dancing with his wife.

"Everybody loves you!" Monica Schloss said gaily. She tapped Maxie on the head on her way out of the room. "Everybody happy?" she asked.

"Everybody's happy," Max said, smiling. She put a hand on her cousin's shoulder. "That was great, Rain," she said.

The boy flashed a grin. "Thanks," he said.

Lingering next to Max on the other side of the piano, Amy shook her head in awe. "That was some of the greatest music I've ever heard," she said. "Max told me you were a talented musician, but talented is not the word. Some of the chords you play—it's like you pull them out of the air."

Rain smiled modestly. "Sometimes that's what it feels like," he said. "Like I'm just up there in the air with the music, know what I mean?"

"I know exactly what you mean," Palmer said loudly. The beautiful blond waltzed past, displaying her turquoise dress. "I'm Max's close friend, Palmer Durand," she said, sticking her hand out.

Rain smiled. "Glad to meet you," he said warmly.

Turning away from Palmer, Rain looked at Amy. "Max tells me you're into music," the boy said with an interested look in his eyes.

"She's very interested in music," Palmer volunteered,

116

leaning into the piano. "I ought to know because she's my roommate. As a matter of fact," she added, "I'm into music myself."

"You into music?" Max said with a giggle. "That's the opposite of what you said this afternoon."

"That was because I hadn't heard Rain yet," Palmer piped up. Nudging her way in front of Max, Palmer batted her eyes.

Rain played softly while Amy listened.

"That's the riff," Amy said enthusiastically. "How did you think of that?"

"What can I say?" Rain said with a friendly smile. "My head is just filled with them. Come here"— he beckoned to Amy—"listen to this."

As Palmer stood jealously by, the handsome boy made room for Amy on the bench in front of the piano.

"He's not paying any attention to me," Palmer complained, rejoining Shanon. "It's not like Amy to be so boy-crazy!"

"Look who's talking," Shanon giggled.

"What's this?" Max asked, joining the huddle.

"I think your cousin is the cutest boy I've ever seen in my entire life," Palmer confessed, "and Amy's hogging him. Why doesn't she go find her date?"

"There he is now," Max pointed out as Alex Ho walked toward the piano and stood next to his sister. "Now she's got two boys," Palmer pouted.

Max laughed. "My cousin Rain is discussing music with Amy, that's all."

Shanon, Palmer, and Max stood by as Rain played softly and Amy hummed. Alex observed his sister with gleaming eyes.

"I'm going upstairs to put on some more makeup," Palmer announced impulsively. "I'm sure I ate off my lip-

117

stick when I was eating that hoagie." She jabbed Max in the side. "Don't let your cousin go anywhere."

"Okay, Palmer," Max said, rolling her eyes.

Sharing a look of amusement, Shanon and Max came in closer. Rain and Amy were still having a conversation.

"So do you write music?" Rain asked her.

Amy shrugged self-consciously. "A little."

"Don't be modest," Alex said, joining in. "Amy's hot."

Amy turned and blushed. "Thanks, Alex."

Max touched her cousin's shoulder. "Want some punch, Rain?" she asked.

"Thanks, Max," he said. "I could use it before the next set."

While Max disappeared into the other room for Rain's drink, Shanon moved in a bit closer.

"Amy's a great song writer," she volunteered.

Rain smiled and gave Amy a sidelong glance. "That's the third good thing I've heard about you," he teased. "I've got to hear you."

Amy shook her head violently. "No, I couldn't," she said. Even though most people had gone into the food room, some of the crowd was still in there.

"Come on, Amy," Alex prodded. He ruffled his sister's hair. "Sing that one you wrote the other day."

"You wrote a new song?" Shanon said brightly. "I'd like to hear it, too."

"Command performance, Amy," Rain teased.

Max came back with Rain's punch. "What's happening?" she asked. "Aren't you going to take a break?"

"Not until I hear one of Amy's songs," Rain said lightly.

Amy looked at her friends and at Max's cousin. Part of her really, really wanted to sing her song, but a big part of her was scared. What if Rain Blackburn thought her lyrics were corny? What if he thought her melodies were too

118

childish? The songs that she thought up were certainly not as sophisticated as the ones he'd played a little while ago.

"Hum a little for me," Rain said. He laid his hands on the keys.

In spite of her fear, Amy hummed. "That's it . . ." she said as Rain picked up the melody. "It's for this new song I just wrote, 'In My Too Quiet House.' "

"Sing a little," said Rain.

Smiling shyly, Amy glanced around the room, then in a soft voice she sang her new song. "Terrible two's . . . terrible teens . . . the voice, the face of my soul . . ." Even though she was singing softly, with Rain's wonderful playing in the background, Amy felt her soul soar. If only she could be a real musician like him someday. Before she realized it, she had sung her new song to the end. Alex, Max, and Shanon applauded, as did a few other people.

"If that's an example of your work," Rain said encouragingly, "I say you should keep going."

Amy rolled her eyes. "My parents would drop dead if I took that advice."

"But you're good," Alex said, still standing behind her. "You're talented—isn't she?" he asked Rain, Max, and Shanon.

"I think so," Max said.

"Me, too," said Shanon.

"You see?" said Alex, beaming at his sister.

"I like your style, too," Rain said to Amy. Behind his wire-rimmed glasses, his eyes twinkled mysteriously. "When I was nine years old, I told everybody my world was music," he said softly. "My dad said to get out of here, kid—you're gonna be a doctor!" Rain laughed. "Maybe I will be a doctor someday, but right now the only thing for me is playing the piano. What can I say? It's what gives me joy."

"I know what you mean," Amy said earnestly.

"Then go for it," Rain said, getting up from the piano. "Excuse me, my break's nearly over. I'm going upstairs to splash my face with some water."

"Check on my brothers while you're there, will you?" said Max. "The last time I saw them they were in their room. You know how they can be."

"Right," Rain said, saluting them playfully.

"He is awesome!" Amy breathed when Max's cousin was out of hearing.

"He's also very sweet," Max said proudly.

"He certainly liked your music, Amy," said Shanon.

Amy shrugged. "Well, yeah, he did say so," she admitted, grinning.

"That's because you're good," Alex said, playfully squeezing her shoulder.

Amy touched her brother's hand. It hadn't been so bad having him come to the party with her after all. "Thanks," she said, giving him a smile.

Max took Shanon aside and whispered mischievously, "Amy and her date with the 'mohawk' really like each other!"

Suddenly Shanon felt someone else next to her. It was the woman in the silvery evening dress, Faline Trudeau. She smiled at Shanon warmly.

"Do you think we could talk?" the woman asked kindly.

"Are you talking to me?" Shanon asked in surprise.

Max put an arm around her friend's shoulder. "Have you met my roommate, Faline?"

"Yes, we have met," the woman said, flashing a beautiful smile. "I'd like to have a chat with you, Shanon," she said, "if you have a minute."

"Don't mind me," said Max, backing away.

"Thanks, Maxie," said Ms. Trudeau. "By the way, as

always your parents are throwing a fabulous party."

"Yes, it's great," Max agreed with a wave. "I'm going into the living room to see to my other guests."

Shanon was left alone with the owner of the modeling agency. She felt flustered by the woman's attention. "Did you, uh, want to talk to me about something special?" she asked.

"In a way," Ms. Trudeau replied. She laid a gentle hand on Shanon's arm. "Let's find a cozy spot where it's quiet." She led Shanon over to a window seat, and they sat down. "Have you ever thought of modeling?" Faline asked, with a smile.

"M-me?" Shanon stammered.

"Yes, you," said Faline, studying Shanon. "Your face has a wonderfully natural look. It's fresh."

"Thanks a lot," said Shanon.

"I think other people would agree with me," said the owner of the modeling agency. "In fact, I think you have the kind of fresh natural look editors are looking for. . . ."

CHAPTER FIFTEEN

———◆———

While Amy, Alex, Max, and Shanon were downstairs, Palmer was in Max's bedroom putting on more lip gloss. Her heart was still racing from having met Rain Blackburn.

Rain looked really old—he was probably sixteen! thought Palmer excitedly. If he was in Max's family, he was probably rich. And if he was such a good musician at the age of sixteen, someday he'd probably be famous. If only there was some way she could get his attention!

"I wonder what kind of car he drives," she wondered as she ran a quick brush through her hair. Not that it *really* mattered. Maybe Max would invite Rain along the following day when they went sight-seeing! Maybe he'd drive them instead of the chauffeur. Rain probably had a BMW or a Jaguar! She'd have to make sure she was sitting right in the front seat next to Rain. She'd arrange that beforehand with Maxie.

Satisfied with her image, Palmer turned to leave. Her mind was filled with fantasies! She had a plan—she'd find some way of getting Amy's attention, then she'd trade places with her roommate and sit next to Rain on the piano bench! When he stopped playing, she'd ask him about himself. She'd think of something musical to talk about. Certainly, she'd heard enough talk about music from Sam O'Leary. Thinking of her pen pal, she had an instant pang of guilt, but it lasted only an instant. Sam wasn't here and Rain Blackburn was. It certainly wasn't her fault if Rain should happen to like her.

Turning on her heel to the door, she came to a screeching stop. Something small, green, and slimy-looking was blocking her way. "Oh!" she screamed. "It's a frog!" Startled, she jumped backward. Palmer was afraid of anything slimy. "How in the world did a frog get in Max's room?" she gulped. Behind her she heard a loud "ribbet." Whirling around, she saw a second even larger frog on one of the flowered coverlets. Then, on the windowsill, she caught sight of a third. "They're all over the place!" she said, gasping in horror. "I've got to get out of here! What am I going to do?" There was only one thing to do—run! But the first frog she'd discovered was still guarding the door. Flinging herself across the room, Palmer made a big leap. To think she'd been in Max's bedroom putting on makeup all this time with a bunch of frogs watching her. She'd been so busy looking at herself in the mirror she hadn't even noticed.

"Gross!" she yelled, lunging out of the doorway. "Gross, disgusting! Gross! Disgusting, slimy creatures—I hate you! Gross!"

At that moment, Rain Blackburn was walking down the corridor. Palmer nearly leapt into his arms.

"Is something wrong?" he asked in surprise. He gave her a quizzical grin. "Maybe I should call The Ghostbusters."

Palmer was breathless. "I . . . I . . . there's frogs . . ." she stammered. This wasn't the way she'd planned to meet Max's cousin! "Little green things, all over Max's room,"

123

she groaned. Rain stepped away and Palmer followed. "It's a good thing you came along," she said quickly.

Rain stepped up to the door and picked up the frog.

"Yuk!" Palmer couldn't help moaning.

"What's wrong?" Rain asked mischievously. "Who knows—this little froggie might be a handsome prince in disguise."

Palmer smoothed her hair, trying to recover herself. The only "handsome prince" on the premises was Rain. "I . . . I like your music," she stammered, keeping her distance from the amphibian.

"Thanks," said Rain with a twinkle in his eyes. "I'm glad you do."

Just then they heard loud giggles. Max's brothers were hiding in the hall.

"It was them!" she accused, spying the boys. "They're horrible! To think they put those slimy things in Max's room. One was even on the bedspread! I hope they don't get into my suitcase."

Rain turned to his young cousins. Peeking from behind the potted palm where they'd been hiding, the "monster pip-squeaks" were in stitches.

"What's wrong, Palmer," the oldest one Gary teased, "don't you like animals?"

"No, I don't," Palmer huffed. She glanced at Rain. "I mean, I don't especially like frogs," she said, batting her eyes. She didn't want Rain to think she was an animal hater in case he loved them.

Rain gestured to his three younger cousins. "Come on, boys," he said, peering into Maxie's room, "you've got some rounding up to do. Get those froggies!"

"It was Brian's idea," lisped Kevin apologetically. "He thought the frogs needed some company."

"Ha, ha," Palmer said sarcastically. She smiled softly at Rain. "They really are little rascals," she giggled, trying to cover up her feelings. In fact, she felt like wringing the boys' necks, and she also wished they'd get lost. Her golden opportunity to get to know Rain was being wasted talking about frogs!

"Maybe I should supervise this," Rain said, glancing at the staircase. "My aunt Monica will be awfully upset if these things get downstairs."

Palmer nodded in agreement. "I would say I'd help you," she volunteered weakly, "but you seem to be an expert."

Rain laughed and stroked the frog he was holding. The three boys had already gone inside. "What can I say?" Rain chuckled. "I like frogs."

"Oh, I like frogs, too!" Palmer blurted out with a blush. "I mean I love them. I mean it was just a bit of a shock to find them watching me put on my makeup."

Rain watched her with a twinkle in his eyes. Palmer felt a shiver. Max's cousin seemed definitely intrigued.

"We've got them all, Rain," Gary announced, coming out of Maxie's room. The three boys lined up holding their frogs.

"Great," Rain said, giving them the last frog. "Now if you'll excuse me—I've got another set to play," he added, hurrying to the staircase.

"Can I go with you?" Palmer asked, catching up.

"Sure," Rain said casually. "Keep me company."

Palmer practically floated downstairs. She took a seat next to Rain on the piano bench.

As the room began to rock again with Rain's music, and dancers gathered on the floor, Palmer shut her eyes and sighed. *You never know how you'll meet the boy of your dreams!* she thought. *Maybe I'll even get to like frogs.*

125

Max, Amy, and Alex stood by the French doors. Her conversation with Faline Trudeau finished, Shanon joined them.

"Looks like Palmer has nabbed your cousin," Shanon reported gaily. Her face was beaming.

"I can't believe it!" Amy exclaimed, turning around. She bobbed her head in time to the music. "I'm glad Rain is playing again. This is a great night."

Max came up next to Shanon. "What was Faline talking to you about all that time?" she asked confidentially.

Shanon produced a small white card. "She gave me this card with her telephone number on it," Shanon said, blushing with pleasure. "You won't believe this, but she thinks I could be a model."

"Great!" said Amy.

"You are very pretty," Alex added sweetly.

"I had a feeling she might be scouting you out!" Max said with excitement. "Faline was watching you all night."

Shanon laughed. "Palmer made sure I was seen."

"What did you tell her?" Max asked eagerly.

"I said I wasn't interested," Shanon replied.

"Why?" asked Max in surprise.

Shanon shrugged and smiled. "I'm just not the model type," she said simply.

Max leaned against the window overlooking the balcony. "Anybody hungry?" she asked. "We've got these great pastries."

"I might try one, before I hit the road," said Alex. He poked Amy. "Mom and Dad are letting you stay the night, right?"

"Right!" Amy sighed. "I'm free!"

"Lucky you, sis," he said, "that means it'll only be me they're waiting up for tonight."

"Hey, what's going on?" Max asked, overhearing.

"Yes . . ." said Shanon, also bewildered.

"Why did Alex call you sis?" Max demanded.

"And why are your mom and dad going to be waiting up for him?" Shanon asked suspiciously.

"Uh-oh . . ." said Alex, hitting his head.

Amy looked away. "The cat's out of the bag, I guess," she mumbled, hanging her head. "Shanon, Max—meet my brother."

Alex grinned and stroked his mohawk. "Surprise—didn't mean to crash your party."

"Wait a minute here," said Max, breaking up.

"I'll explain later," Amy hedged. "Okay, I lied. I admit it," she said, laughing.

Shanon looked at Alex and then at Amy. "I should've known there was something about you that was familiar."

Alex grinned widely. "Must be the mohawk! Hey, neat," he added, pointing outside. "I didn't even see that before."

"See what?" Max asked, squinting out of the window.

"Out there with the reindeer," Alex remarked. "You've got a mechanical Santa."

"Let me see that!" Max exclaimed, pressing her nose to the glass.

"He really does look lifelike," Shanon said, startled.

"Yeah, wow," Amy said. "Standing next to those reindeer, he looks like the real thing."

The "mechanical" Santa started to wave at them. A huge voice boomed out, "Ho, ho, ho . . . Merry Christmas, Happy New Year! This is a recorded announcement. Ho, ho, ho. . . ."

"Oh, no!" Max wailed. "It's my father! What a riot, ha, ha! He couldn't resist!"

"Incredible!" laughed Amy.

"Awesome," Alex said, doubling over.

127

"It's really funny," giggled Shanon.

"Come on," said Max. "Mom's serving pastries."

Gathering around the piano once more the foursome joined Palmer and Rain. Palmer's eyes were glued on the piano player. Monica Schloss came by with a tray of pastries.

The room was jumping again. Mr. Schloss came in from the cold through the French doors and danced in his snow-covered Santa suit. The "pip-squeaks" made another appearance, but seemed to be calmer. Shanon sat on the window seat, taking it all in.

"Having a good time?" Monica Schloss asked softly, swishing by in her dress.

"Yes, thanks," Shanon said, with stars in her eyes. She pressed the card from Faline Trudeau between her palms. *Anything can happen in New York!* she thought.

And the party went on. . . .

CHAPTER SIXTEEN

"I can't believe that Faline Trudeau actually asked you to call her!" Palmer exclaimed with just a hint of jealousy.

The party was over and the four girls were getting ready for bed in Maxie's room.

"I was kind of shocked myself," Shanon confessed shyly.

"Humph," said Palmer slyly. "I wonder if she's going to call me."

"You're so conceited!" Max teased, rolling her eyes. The gangly redhead was fluffing up pillows. "It's Shanon that Faline's interested in, not you, Palmer."

"Faline Trudeau told Shanon that she was a fresh new face," Amy reported, giving Shanon a wink. Sitting down on her cot, she cautiously lifted a pillow. "I just hope there aren't any more frogs in here."

"None in my bed," Max announced, shaking her bed-spread. "And I checked out Palmer's, and Shanon's."

"Thanks," Shanon muttered, rummaging in her suitcase. "I don't mind frogs, but I'd hate to sleep with them."

"I mind frogs whether I'm awake or asleep," Palmer said, tissuing off her makeup at the mirror. "Of course, this evening frogs were my lucky amphibians."

Amy howled. "Lucky amphibians!"

"Well, my lucky charms then," Palmer sputtered. "Whatever you want to call them, frogs are what brought me and Rainer together."

Max smothered a giggle. "Rainer? He told you his first name is actually Rainer? My cousin hates that name! That's why everyone calls him Rain."

Palmer's cheeks tinged pink. "We were having a discussion about names after he finished playing," she reported defensively. "I told him my middle name was Stuyvesant, and he told me his real first name was Rainer. I think Rainer is a very dignified name," Palmer announced, drawing herself up. She gazed at her reflection in the mirror. "This is a date I will always remember—it might be the most important night in my life."

Amy whistled. "She's got it bad."

"Sure does," agreed Shanon, "and in such a short time."

"Romeo and Juliet fell in love in an instant," Palmer protested. "When I walked into the room and saw Rain at the piano"—she clutched her heart—"I had a feeling that was indescribable."

"Gee," Max said softly, "that's poetic. Does Rain feel the same way about you?"

"I'm sure he does," Palmer said earnestly. "I mean, if I feel that way about him, he must feel that way about me!"

"Did he tell you that?" Shanon asked.

Palmer sat down on her cot. "Not in so many words, but the way he looked at me when the frogs were being collected . . . it was so romantic!"

Amy giggled. "Boy, when collecting frogs is romantic— you really are in love."

"That's just it," Palmer said earnestly. "I think I am."

"But what about Sam O'Leary?" Shanon asked, creeping closer.

130

Palmer tossed her head. "What about Sam?"

"You told us he was your boyfriend when you arrived today," Max reminded her.

"I hope you're not going to dump him," said Shanon. "Sam's so nice, and he's been such a good pen pal."

"Of course I'm not going to dump him," Palmer said impatiently. "Not right away anyway. Is there any law that says I can't be in love with Rain and keep writing to Sam? There was another boy I liked in L.A. also," she added enthusiastically. "His name is Frankie, but I wasted my time even thinking about him," she finished up quickly.

"You've had a heavy vacation in the boy department," Amy said, flopping down on Max's bed.

Palmer took a thin book out of her overnight bag. "Read all about it in my journal," she said smugly. "I wrote so much, mine must be the longest."

"Our journals!" Shanon exclaimed. "I'd almost forgotten about them!" She ran to get hers from her suitcase, while Max got her own out of her desk.

"Should we trade tonight or tomorrow?" Shanon asked excitedly.

"Tomorrow," Amy said stubbornly, "because I didn't bring mine."

"Aww, why not?" asked Max.

"Because it's too embarrassing to let you know how my parents treat me," Amy confessed, "and that's all I wrote about."

"Were they very strict?" Shanon asked sympathetically.

"More than ever," Amy complained. She eyed Max. "I never told you about that part of my life. Even Palmer would have been surprised at how much they treated me like a baby this time," she added.

"I'm surprised," said Max. "You're such a free person, I thought your parents gave you ultimate freedom."

131

Amy chortled. "Believe me—they don't! Why do you think Alex came with me this evening?"

"It was kind of unusual that your date turned out to be your brother," Shanon chuckled good-naturedly.

"You really had me fooled!" Max exclaimed.

"Sorry I lied," Amy said sheepishly.

"You should be," Palmer scolded. "I'm surprised that I didn't recognize Alex. You've shown me his picture before."

"He didn't have a mohawk haircut in the picture," Amy giggled. "Besides," she added mischievously, "you were too busy watching Max's cousin to notice my brother."

"True," said Palmer, motioning Shanon to unzip her dress. "I'm sleepy," she said with a yawn. "I'm going to put on my nightgown."

"I'm going to put on my pajamas, too," announced Max.

"If only my parents could treat me like a normal fourteen-year-old," Amy mumbled, diving into her suitcase. She took off her dress and tossed it in. "They didn't even let me get my ears pierced. Someday I'll show them who I really am."

"Someday you might be a famous rock 'n' roll star," Shanon said sympathetically. She sat down on the edge of Amy's bed.

"Yes, Rain thought Amy was incredibly talented," Max piped up. Heading for the bathroom, she came back with her toothbrush. "I heard Rain say that Amy should 'go for it.' " She shrugged and giggled. "Whatever that means!"

"It was really sweet of your cousin," Amy said. She shimmied into one of the oversize T-shirts she slept in. "I can't really 'go for it' in a professional way while I'm in school. But I can keep working on my style, so that when

132

I get out of school . . ." Her black eyes gleamed. "Someday I'll do it," she vowed, "and I'll remember Rain's advice."

Palmer put her hands on her hips. "Just a minute—you sound as if *you're* in love with Max's cousin!"

Amy opened her mouth wide indignantly. "Of course not! Rain may be incredibly cute, but I'm only interested in his musical side."

"Great," Palmer mumbled, tossing her dress over a chair, "because I'm interested in the other sides of him— you know, his personality and looks, etc."

"His allowance," Amy teased, "his car . . ."

"Does Rain have a car?" Palmer inquired of Max.

Max nodded. "A BMW. His dad bought it for him. They live out in the suburbs."

"Oh my gosh!" Palmer gasped. "Something told me that he drove a great car like that! Do you think we could see him tomorrow?" she begged. "He could take us sight-seeing!"

"I don't know about that," Max said hesitantly. "Rain may have other plans. He has lots of girlfriends."

"That's why we have to invite him to go with us, to-morrow," insisted Palmer.

Shanon yawned and sighed, "Poor Sam. . . ."

The girls finished getting ready for bed. Like Palmer, Shanon wore a nightgown, only hers was red flowered flannel instead of white cotton.

"If nobody else has anything to bring up," Max said, once they were settled, "I'd like to run a situation by you that's been on my mind."

She picked up her journal. The letters she'd received from Jose were sticking out. "I showed these letters to Shanon already," she said, handing Amy and Palmer each a letter. "Jose had a rotten Christmas."

Amy and Palmer took a moment to read.

133

"Certainly sounds like it," Amy said, trading letters with Palmer.

"Poor guy," Palmer said. "I was complaining because I only got half my Christmas list. And that dumb doll I hate so much is probably the one that Jose's little sister really wanted."

"What doll are you talking about?" Shanon asked curiously.

"I wrote about it in my journal," Palmer reported. "In fact, I've got it with me. I wanted to leave the doll in California, but in the end I decided that would be too rude. You see, the doll was a gift from my dad."

"A doll from your dad?" Max said, with her eyes widening.

"Where did he get the idea you were into dolls?" asked Amy.

"Oh, a little bird told him," Palmer answered sarcastically.

Hopping off of the cot, she ran to the closet. She wrested the giant doll from a canvas zippered bag. "Isn't this the silliest thing you've ever seen?" she announced.

Amy and Max burst out laughing.

"It's got your name on it!" squealed Max.

"Instead of a Barbie doll, you got a Palmer doll," giggled Amy.

"I think it's kind of wonderful," Shanon said quietly.

"For a four-year-old," Palmer agreed, straightening the doll's sweater.

"It certainly would make some little girl happy," Shanon said thoughtfully. She turned to Max. "Maybe Palmer could give it to Jose's sister."

"What a neat idea," Max said brightly. "How about it, Palmer?"

Palmer shrugged. "Why not? I think it must have cost a fortune, but it's for a good cause."

"Hmm," Max said thoughtfully. "If we give a big present like this to Becky, we'll have to give something to the other kids."

"Otherwise they might feel left out," Amy agreed.

"I could donate some ice skates, too," Palmer piped up. "I have a pair my mom gave me a few years ago I've hardly used. They might fit a kid's foot."

"Billy could at least try them on," said Maxie excitedly. "Now, if we could only think of some other things."

"What was the other stuff the kids wanted?" Amy asked, scanning Jose's letter.

"Some books," said Max.

"I've got plenty of books," Shanon said. "Doreen and I cleaned out our room and I know my little brothers don't need all of them!"

"Wow," said Max. "There's probably lots of stuff we could give the Hurt children, if we could just collect it all. Come to think of it, I know that Jose really wanted a microscope. He told me so the last time I saw him in the library. He just didn't write it down. My brother Gary got a new microscope for Christmas and his old one is almost like new!"

"Bingo!" said Amy. "There's Jose's microscope!"

Max sat up on her bed cross-legged. "The problem is when are we going to give it to him? The holidays are almost over. It won't be as much fun if we give the kids their presents in January."

"It sounds to me like these kids really wanted Santa Claus to give it to them, anyway," declared Amy.

Palmer's blue eyes sparkled. "Maybe we could hire Max's father for a day," she suggested. "Standing out on

135

the lawn this evening, he looked totally authentic."

"Don't remind me," Max said, throwing her hands over her face. "And don't bring up the subject of monster pipsqueaks, either! I could wring my brothers' necks for planting those frogs in my room!"

"Don't be sorry about the frogs," Amy said mischievously. "Frogs are Palmer's lucky amphibians!"

Shanon got up and looked out of the window. She was still thinking of Jose. Since her family often struggled to make ends meet, she had a good idea of how he felt.

"Suppose we all go back to school early and give them a party?" Shanon suggested, turning around. "We could give them kind of a late Christmas!"

"Cool idea." Max said in surprise, "but how? . . ."

"I wouldn't mind going back early," Amy said, jumping on the idea. "I'm dying to go back."

"I'm sure my mom wouldn't mind my going back to school early," said Palmer. She giggled. "She thinks I can use all the exposure to school I can get."

"This idea is shaping up," Amy said excitedly. "My dad's company imports zillions of little toys. Just the kind that kids like! They cost him practically nothing. If we could get him to donate some of them . . ."

"And I'll contribute the doll and the ice skates," Palmer added.

"I can get Ollie to drive it all up in the car!" Max exclaimed, jumping up.

"Except my Florida stuff," objected Palmer. "I can bring that on the airplane."

"And I'm right there in Brighton," said Shanon. "My dad will drive me over with the books. Not only that, Nana and I can bake some cookies."

"Uh-oh," Max said. "We forgot one thing—Maggie and Dan might not want us back early in the dorm."

"And Jose's family might be busy," Shanon said.

"But we can still try to arrange things," Amy said hopefully. "Maybe we should write Maggie and Dan tonight."

"No time," Max said with authority. "We'll call them tomorrow. But first we'll get in touch with Jose. And then we'll ask our parents right away. The vacation's practically over anyway. How could they say no to our giving a party for Jose?"

"Plus your dad's taking us ice skating tomorrow," Amy added. "It's going to be a busy morning!"

Palmer eyed Shanon across the room. "Are you going to call Faline Trudeau tomorrow?" she asked.

"I'm sure Ollie could take you over to her office if Faline wants to interview you," Max volunteered helpfully. "You could see Faline after we go ice skating at Rockefeller Center."

"I told you I wasn't interested," Shanon hedged.

"Well, *I* would be interested," Palmer said bluntly. "In fact, why don't you give the card to me?"

"I think I'll hold on to it for a while," Shanon said firmly.

"Why?" Palmer wanted to know.

"Just because . . ." said Shanon.

Max had taken out her journal.

"What are you writing?" asked Amy.

"A list of refreshments for Jose's party," said Max.

"You talk as if you know it'll work out," said Shanon.

Max grinned. "I'm going to do everything that I can to see that it does work out."

"Your inviting us to *this* party certainly did," Palmer said, lying down on her bed.

"Yes, thanks for inviting us," Shanon said.

"You're a wild and wacky woman!" Amy said. She did a cartwheel across the room. "Your parties are wild and wacky too! Look—I'm not even sleepy!"

137

Shanon smiled sadly. "If only Lisa had made it—"

Max tapped her head and jumped off the bed. "What a klutz!" she exclaimed. Dashing over to her dresser, she opened the top drawer. "I put this in here so I wouldn't forget, and then I forgot about it!" Running past Shanon's cot, she dropped a thin book.

"What's that?" Shanon asked.

"Lisa's journal," Max said, smiling broadly. "It came in the mail yesterday. I thought you'd want to be the first to read it," she added kindly.

Shanon clutched the book and smiled. "I'll read it on the train back to New Hampshire," she murmured.

"Look!" Amy called from the other side of the room. She was looking out of Max's front window. "It's snowing again."

The other three girls joined her and peeked out. The blanketed city street was still lit up with lights. And above was a very faint, eerie moon.

"Look at all the lights that are still on!" exclaimed Shanon.

"It is incredible," agreed Palmer. "It's three o'clock in the morning."

Max squeezed Amy's shoulder. "It's the city that 'never sleeps' as the song goes, right?"

"Right," Amy said, grinning wryly.

The Foxes stood for a while, watching the snow. Shanon was still holding Lisa's journal. One more half day in New York City for Shanon and Palmer, a brief visit back home, and then before anyone could say "the cow jumped over the moon," they'd be back together again in Fox Hall.

CHAPTER SEVENTEEN

Lisa McGreevy—Fox "in absentia." Her journal.

Dear Shanon, Amy, Palmer, and Max,

I hope you don't mind, but my "journal" is in the form of a big letter to you. The main reason I decided to write down what happened to me over Christmas vacation was to share it with you. But unfortunately I'm not used to keeping a regular diary. After the first day, I kind of forgot to write very much! So, here in the longest letter you'll ever get in your lives is "what I did on Christmas vacation!" (smile!)

First, let me say that I was sorry not to be able to make it to Max's party. I have heard so much about Max from Shanon's letters that I really feel like I know her. And it has been so long since I've seen Shanon, Amy, and Palmer! Do the three of you look the same as you did last year? I have a picture of you on my dresser—it's a copy of the one that Kate Majors took of the Foxes of the Third Dimension when we first started rooming together at Alma. It seems like such a long time ago. Amy had a punk haircut—does she still wear her hair like that? Does she still like to look "different" and wear black leather pants? That's the way I remember Amy, anyway. I'm sure Palmer looks just as much like a model as she did last year, and that my old roommate Shanon is just as sweet. Even though I haven't got a picture of Max on my dresser, I do have one in my mind. Shanon said that your hair is red and so thick that sometimes you look like a lioness! Wow!

Enough blabbing. 'Cause I know you want to get the goods on my vacation. To put it in a nutshell, it was WEIRD but GREAT.

The weird part has to do with my mother and father. As you know it's the very first Christmas that my family has been separated. You notice that I didn't say that my mom and dad were separated, but that my "family" was separated. That's because that's the way it is in my house. Dad and Mom's marital problems and Dad's decision to move out "for a while" have affected me and Reggie so much that we have also taken sides against each other. Reggie's on my dad's side. And I'm on my mom's. Sounds disgusting, doesn't it?

The holidays are a time when you want to be happy and carefree and have everything the way you remember it from the last year. Little did I think that last Christmas when Mom and Dad, and my grandmother Gammy, and Reggie, and me were all sitting at the table eating Christmas turkey like always, that this year on Christmas we'd be in different places from one another and eating pizza and hot dogs. Oh, Mom and Gammy still had turkey, even though it was in a restaurant. But Reggie and I had pizza and hot dogs in my dad's new apartment with Kristin. Kristin is my dad's girlfriend. Yep, folks, a lot has gone down. Not only has my dad moved to a place on the other side of town, he's been dating another woman. And he chose Christmas Day to tell me and Reggie about it. Needless to say, this did not make for a very merry Christmas as far as I was concerned. All I could think of was my poor mother, who is heartbroken over her separation from my father, sitting somewhere in a restaurant with Gammy eating turkey that was probably roasted in a microwave. Reggie, for some mysterious reason, did not see it this way. Unlike me, he did not refuse to eat the hot dogs and pizza at Dad's apartment, but made a perfect hog out of himself. And later my brother told me he thought Kristin was "stimulating" and that Dad had made a good choice in getting her as a girlfriend. Kristin is a philosophy professor at the college, though she doesn't look a bit intelligent. Furthermore, she is at least ten years younger than Dad. I will never, ever get used to it. My brother says I should lighten up. Anyway, to finish Christmas Day . . . After Dad and Kristin served us dinner (they thought Reggie and I would like all kinds of "kid" food for Christmas, like the pizza, hot dogs, cheddar cheese popcorn, sodas, and other junk food!) they gave us presents. Actually, the presents were from Dad, but Kristin was sitting there smiling as if she had helped pick them out. I have to say that the gifts were wrapped beautifully. I know that my dad wasn't responsible for that. At home, wrapping Christmas presents was always something that Mom and I did—except for the ones going to me of course. I got a couple of huge boxes and I was excited to open them. Inside one was a handwoven backpack from Guatemala. It has all these gorgeous colors in it and lots of room. In summer I'm sure it will be cool on my back, as it's all cotton. My dad thought of it because I like to bike a lot and go on long excursions to sketch. He thought the pack would be a handy way to carry my sketching materials and lunch and something to drink. It really was thoughtful. The other present was an

141

incredibly beautiful light yellow silk dress with a butterfly print on it. The first thing I thought was how well it would go with the butterfly barrette that was in the box Shanon sent me that I opened on Christmas Eve. A funny thing happened, though, when I opened these two great presents. Instead of screaming "yaah!" and lunging at my father to give him a big bear hug (this is what I would have ordinarily done), I started to cry. And everybody just sat there, looking shocked. To tell the truth, I was shocked myself. I hadn't planned on crying. I'm so mad at my dad that I don't want to share anything with him, not even my feelings. But so much has happened in the past few months that I guess a lot of tears had been stored up inside. So when I opened the box with the butterfly dress, a huge lump filled my throat. I tried to swallow it down, but I couldn't. Then the tears started. I tried to stop them, but I couldn't. The next thing I knew I opened my mouth and this crying came out. All I can remember after that is crying and crying, and seeing Kristin and Reggie leave the room to play a computer game. (Dad and Kristin gave Reggie a couple of complicated and "stimulating" computer games that he was thrilled with!) Then I remember seeing my dad looking kind of helpless. I guess I must have cried for about half an hour. Dad kept trying to touch me and I kept saying don't! Yukk! And a Merry Christmas to you, too! That night I went to sleep right away, not even telling my mom what had happened at first. Then I woke up at three o'clock in the morning with a huge pain in my stomach. Don't worry, I didn't have appendicitis or anything dramatic. It was only hunger, since I'd stubbornly passed up the pizza and hot dogs at Dad's.

I was surprised to see a light on downstairs in the kitchen. I thought that I would be alone at three A.M., so I had brought my latest letter from Rob with me. I had only read it about eight times a day since I'd received it, but I wanted to read it once more. All through this time when Mom and Dad have been separated, I have to say that what has pulled me through in my darkest moments has been the mail I've received from my pen pal. And of course, it goes without saying that Shanon's letters have meant just as much! Rob's letters have been very special, too, though. Especially now that I'm in Chestnut High. At the beginning of the year, I thought that things were going to be fine here—there are lots of nice boys and girls. The trouble is, however, that I haven't become friends with many of them. The place is full of cliques, and a lot of the boys think I'm a snob since I used to go to boarding school. There are so many parties—most of which I'm not invited to. And then when I am invited, I'm supposed to bring a boy along. Even if there was a boy who liked me and I liked at Chestnut High, I would find it so embarrassing to ask him to go to a party! I wouldn't be embarrassed to ask Rob. A million times I've wished that Rob were here with me. It's only a dream, though. I know it's not possible.

Like I was starting to tell you before I began to talk about Rob, I was starving to death so I went down to the kitchen. A light was on already because my mother was there in her pajamas. It was the middle of the night and she was up drinking tea.

"Reggie told me that you were upset today," Mom said. She gave me a sympathetic smile. I gulped. Oh, no! I thought. If she's nice to me and treats me like a baby, I might start crying all over again!

"It was okay," I mumbled. I glanced at my mom on the way to the refrigerator. She had bags under her eyes and she hadn't taken off her earrings even though she was in her pajamas. I thought that was peculiar. "How was your dinner with Gammy?" I asked.

"Quite nice," she said cheerfully. She took off one of her earrings. "Your dad gave me these the first Christmas we were married," she said with a soft chuckle. "I don't know what possessed me to pull them out of my jewelry box this morning."

I sighed. *Poor Mom,* I thought. She definitely is miserable. I wondered if she'd heard about Kristin.

"What did you think of Dad's girlfriend?" she asked. This is just like my mother—she often seems to read my thoughts.

"She was okay," I grunted. "Kind of childish. She served us junk food."

Mom smiled at me knowingly. "Reggie enjoyed it."

"That's Reggie," I said, swinging over to the table, sloshing some milk on the way. Reggie is Reggie; I'm me. For example, when it came down that my parents' marriage was on the rocks, my brother just accepted it. He even went so far as to say that their separation was statistically in order. There were so many broken marriages in America these days, why should our family be an exception? That's the way my intellectual brother thinks. So, now on the first Christmas that our family isn't together, and my dad decides to spring it on his kids that there's another woman in his life, all Reggie can say to my mom is that the junk food was good.

Mom reached out and patted my hand. I made a face and started drinking my milk.

"I wish I'd had some turkey," that was all I could manage to say.

Mom went to the cabinet and got me some cookies. One of the gold earrings was on the table. I looked at it. After all the arguments that had occurred in the last few months between my parents, it was hard to imagine they were once young and in love with each other. I tried to picture their first Christmas together before they'd had kids, when Dad had given Mom the gold earrings. I tried to picture it, but all I could see was a blank.

"Is that another letter from Rob?" Mom asked curiously. She gave Rob's letter a polite glance, then took off her other earring. By now I guess she recognized my pen pal's handwriting. Even though I'd never read her a whole letter, I sometimes read portions to her.

"It's the letter I got from him a few days ago," I answered.

"The present he sent you for Christmas certainly was useful," said Mom.

(Rob sent me a waist pouch full of peanuts. Useful and kind of funny! He knows how much I like jogging, thus the waist pouch. He also knows what a pig I am when it comes to peanuts. This may seem odd to you, but I consider this useful and funny present also to be romantic, since I can imagine how hard it must have been for him to think of something to give me. He must have spent lots of time thinking about just the right thing and taken some time shopping for the gift, too. I certainly did shop around a lot for the fountain pen and Batman T-shirt I gave him.)

Mom reached for one of the cookies. She had a little gleam in her eyes as if she was plotting something. "Would you like to see him?" she asked.

"See who?" I asked, my mouth full of cookies.

"Why, Rob," Mom replied. "He must be a close friend if you're still writing to him."

I tell you, Foxes, I couldn't believe it! Seeing Rob again is something I dream about every other night! And my

145

mom looked like she had something definite in mind. Did she know something I didn't? Had she been in touch with Rob's parents or something?

"Where would I see Rob?" I asked, trying to be casual, even though I was dying inside.

Mom said simply, "I thought I could call his parents and invite him for the weekend." She shrugged. "He might not be able to come, but it wouldn't hurt to ask."

"Where would he sleep?" I was almost panting from excitement. Could this really come true? Would I actually see Rob Williams in my house?

"He could sleep in Reggie's room," said Mom.

I almost started to cry. "This is so nice of you," I said to my mother.

Mom smiled a really big smile. She really is neat!

"Do you think Rob might like to see you?" she asked gently.

"I think he might," I gulped. "He still writes that he likes me a lot!" I gushed.

"Are you boyfriend and girlfriend?" she asked simply.

I felt my face get red. "We were," I said. "We said that we were last year when I was at Alma Stephens. Is that okay with you?"

Mom chuckled. "Sure. It's natural for boys and girls to like one another when they get to be teenagers. I had lots of boyfriends before I settled down and went steady with Dad."

I felt a cloud pass over me. This made me think of Kristin again. Now my mom and dad were old and weren't even going to be married anymore.

"I hate Dad for what he's done!" I said. I reached out and kissed my mom's cheek. "I don't care if I ever see him again! What's more I think it's totally insensitive of him to make me stay in town the weekend of Max Schloss's party."

"No matter how Dad feels about me, he'll never stop loving you and Reggie," Mom said gently.

"Well, I don't love him!" I said.

"Of course you do," Mom said quietly. "You're only angry with him for a while."

"You bet I'm angry!" I sputtered. Bringing it all up again just made me angrier. "I never thought that my father would go out and get a girlfriend!"

Mom sighed. She looked thoughtful. "Kristin is a very nice and intelligent person," she said.

"You know her?" I said in shock.

"I'd met her earlier, before she and your father got involved," my mom told me.

"Aren't you jealous?" I wanted to know. "Don't you hate her? It's probably her fault that you and Dad aren't together!"

Mom looked tired, but not that upset. "One thing I can say, Lisa, is that what happened between your dad and me is nobody's fault but our own. Having a relationship with Kristin is your dad's business. It has very little to do with the breakup of our marriage, believe me."

I felt confused and frustrated. "Well, at least you're not dating anybody," I muttered.

"Not at the moment," Mom said. "But the day may come when dating is something I'll consider."

I got up from the table and put my plate and glass in the sink. Talking about this stuff makes me crazy. It's not fair for a person my age to have to deal with it—that's what I think!

Mom came up and put her arm around me. She smoothed my hair. "So, shall I call Rob's parents?" she

147

asked. "Seeing one of your old friends might make you feel better."

"Yes," I said, feeling much more cheerful. "I'll call him first thing in the morning, then I'll put you on with his mother and father."

Mom went upstairs and I went to my room, too. Needless to say, I could hardly sleep. I was already thinking about hearing Rob's voice on the phone. I had hardly ever called him before. Our relationship started through letters, so I'm used to writing him. But I'm happy to say that when I called, Rob accepted my invitation right away.

"Would I like to spend the night?" he asked. His voice cracked when he asked me—I swear.

"You'll have to sleep with Reggie," I warned him. "You know what a nerd he is, but he's okay when he sleeps."

"No problem. It will be so great to see you, Lisa," he said softly.

After that I was speechless and I put Mom on the phone. She and Mr. Williams worked everything out—the best thing for their family's schedule was for Rob to come right away! . . . Luckily they were able to make Rob's travel arrangements. Mom told me that Mr. Williams told her that Rob has talked a lot about me and that our friendship must be very special. He was also impressed with how Rob and I keep up with each other in letters.

So, that's how the GREAT part came about over my vacation. Yes, dear Foxes, Rob Williams, my ever-loving pen pal, was actually in my house. He just left late this afternoon. He is even cuter than he used to be. His hair is curlier and darker. His muscles are bigger. His smile is even friendlier, and more than ever I believe he is the only boy for me. We went to the movies. We went cross-country skiing. We even fixed breakfast together (waffles) for Mom and Reggie. He and Reggie got along great. The three of us even got into one of Reggie's computer games. And most importantly, Mom thought Rob was a very special person, just like I do. This was the greatest gift that anyone could have ever given me. When we went to the movies, I wore my butterfly dress and the butterfly clip Shanon gave me (thanks, Shanon!). Rob and I pigged out on peanuts instead of popcorn. Needless to say, in between reaching into the peanut bag, he held my hand a lot. And I held his. And when we were coming back from cross-country skiing (Mom and Reggie were in front of us, so they couldn't see), we kissed. I am still thinking of it. I hadn't seen Rob in so long, I thought maybe we'd lost that special feeling we experienced with one another. But it's still there! I know, like my mom, I may have tons and tons of boyfriends before I grow up and get a job and maybe decide to get married. But right now, there is no person of the opposite sex that I can think of that is more perfect for me than Rob Williams. He is not only a "boyfriend," he is a true friend, who understands me and makes me laugh a lot.

At the moment I'm not even feeling that angry about Dad dating Kristin. I don't like it, but I don't hate Dad as much. This is a weird time in my life, but I guess it can also be a great time. Not great just because I get wonderful surprises like the visit from Rob. But great because I am learning who I am. I'm asking myself a lot of big questions and learning more about who Lisa McGreevy really is and what she stands for.

After Rob left, I went over to see my dad by myself. We had a talk that brought me a little closer to him. I told him that he made me angry, and he said he could understand my having these feelings. That helped. He took me out to a restaurant and we had turkey. Turkey sandwiches, but it was still turkey. Weird how you get attached to traditions—like turkey at Christmas and having your mom and dad be one happy family with you and your brother. Weird how hard it is when traditions end. One thing that will never change is my feelings for you three—Shanon, Amy, and Palmer. I should say for you four, since Max is one of the Foxes, and I look forward to knowing her. Though I may not be at the party, and I'm no longer with you at school, in many moments I'm sure you can feel me thinking about you. This "journal" that is actually a long letter comes with love and good wishes and hope for a great new year for all of us and our families. We're growing up! And sometimes it ain't easy.

Love,
From the Fox numero uno!
Lisa McGreevy

CHAPTER EIGHTEEN

Shanon closed her friend's journal thoughtfully. Since she'd come back home to New Hampshire the night before, she'd read Lisa's journal three times. Still tired out by the trip from New York, Shanon stretched and yawned and stared at the dark circles under her eyes in the mirror. No wonder she had dark circles! She and her suitemates had stayed up till dawn the night of the big party, and the Foxes' second day in the "Big Apple" had by no means been uneventful. First ice skating, then the Christmas show at Radio City Music Hall. Then a late lunch at the Hard Rock Cafe with Maxie's cousin Rain. When Palmer heard Rain was joining them, she was ecstatic!—until Rain walked in with a date! But after she'd got over the shock, Rain's having a date didn't stop Palmer! When the girl went to the ladies' room, Palmer sneaked into the seat Rain's date had been sitting in. Within five minutes she had found out that Rain's grandparents had a home in Palm Beach. This was the perfect excuse for Palmer to slip Rain her Palm Beach telephone number. She scrawled it on a napkin and slid it over to him.

Going over the scene in her mind, Shanon laughed out

loud. Palmer really was something! The afternoon had been so much fun! Even Max's brothers had behaved themselves, and Amy had gone wild over finally going to the Hard Rock.

Dragging herself over to the small closet in her new room, Shanon pulled out her plaid bathrobe. "Better get up sometime," she muttered, stepping into her animal slippers. The vacation was just about over and she'd brought home school work she hadn't even started, not to mention the story ideas Kate was expecting at the *Ledger*'s next editorial meeting after the break. The next day she was going back to school to make the holiday celebration for the Hurt children. "The party's over," Shanon mumbled with a smile to herself. Reaching into the side pouch of her as-yet-unpacked suitcase, Shanon felt her red toothbrush. Also grazing her fingers was the smooth white card Faline Trudeau had left with her. Sticking the toothbrush in her mouth, she gazed at the card thoughtfully.

What a laugh, she thought with a wistful nod of head. Of all the gorgeous young women at Max's party, including some of Max's friends from her old school, not to mention Palmer, Faline Trudeau had asked *her*, Shanon Davis, if she was interested in a modeling career! Rolling her eyes at the thought, Shanon caught sight of herself in the mirror. Dressed as she was in the plaid robe she'd had since she was ten and her hair sticking up like feathers and a toothbrush in her mouth, she hardly looked like "a fresh young face." But the memory of being paid such a compliment by a woman as important as Faline Trudeau was something she'd cherish forever. Carefully, placing the small, white card in the middle of her dresser, she quietly left her room.

After showering and having some oatmeal made by Nana, Shanon looked in on five minutes of cartoons with her little brothers. Then she went to look for her big sister.

Dressed in a heavy ski sweater and bright red headband, Doreen Davis was working behind the counter in the Davis Convenience Store.

"Hey, sleepy head," Doreen joked. "Have a wild and crazy time in the city?"

"Kind of," Shanon admitted sheepishly. "I wish you'd been there."

"I'll get there someday," Doreen said good-naturedly. A customer approached the cash register with a few items. Shanon stood to one side patiently, while Doreen rang up the groceries.

"Have a good day," her sister called out when she'd finished helping the customer. The customer, who was an older woman, smiled back.

"And you too, dear. Thanks for your help."

"You sure are good at this," Shanon said admiringly.

"I've been doing it for enough summers," said Doreen. "Dad decided that since I'm staying at home this semester, I might as well work here," she added cheerfully.

"How long are you going to do that?" Shanon asked.

Doreen shrugged. "Until I get something else," she said. Reaching over the counter, she gave Shanon a package of bubble gum. "On the house—" she said slyly, nabbing a second pack for herself.

Shanon giggled. "One advantage to working in a store owned by your own father," she said. The sisters exchanged a knowing smile. Ever since they'd been little kids, they'd been snitching bubble gum from the family store for each other.

"How are things with Dad?" Shanon asked, hoping that the battle over Doreen's not going back to college had simmered down.

"He's not nagging me as much," Doreen confided. "I think Mom convinced him to let me stew in my own juices for a while." She laughed nervously. "They're probably thinking I'll change my mind and go back to school at the last minute."

"Will you?" asked Shanon.

"I've made up my mind," said Doreen. "Working in the store for Dad and Mom isn't exactly what I want to do, but I'm not going back to college . . . maybe not even the following semester," she added seriously.

Shanon reached into her pocket.

"I brought you a present from New York," she said.

"What is it?" Doreen asked, peering over the counter. "It must be pretty small to fit in your pocket."

Shanon handed over the white card Faline Trudeau had given her. "Big things come in little packages, sometimes," she said meaningfully.

Doreen read the card aloud, "Trudeau Modeling Agency, Faline Trudeau owner. . . ." She shrugged. "What's this mean?"

Shanon's face dimpled. "It means that even though you're not going back to college, you're going to have a career. Or you might have one eventually," she announced, bursting with happiness. "This woman Faline is so nice and so beautiful and very important," Shanon said in a rush. "She told me if I ever wanted a career in modeling—"

"But what does it have to do with me?" Doreen cut in excitedly.

"I'm not interested in being a model," Shanon said, "no matter how fresh Ms. Trudeau thinks my face is. I'd die if I had to stand around in front of a bunch of people getting my picture taken. And as for commercials—forget it! As soon as I got in front of the camera, I'd probably faint. But you, on the other hand—"

"I think you're dumb to turn this woman down if she's actually interested in you," Doreen cut in.

"Well, I did turn her down," Shanon declared. "But I'm not the only one of the family Faline is interested in."

Doreen blushed faintly.

"I told her about you, too," said Shanon. Her eyes brimming with feeling, she faced her big sister. "I told her that you were the prettiest and most unusual-looking person I've ever met, and that you had everything it took to be a real show person. That *you*, Doreen Davis, are the one she's looking for."

Flushing with a mixture of bewilderment and pleasure, Shanon's sister let out a hoot. "If I ever did become a model, I certainly wouldn't need an agent with you around! What did this woman say when you told her about me?"

"She said that you could call her anytime you like," Shanon said. "She said she would talk to you, give you some advice! I told her that you weren't sure what you wanted to do and . . ."

"Whoa," said Doreen. "I appreciate your mentioning me to this woman, but"—she gave Shanon a helpless smile—"people don't just become models overnight."

"Faline was going to try to make me one," Shanon said simply. "Besides, she told me there were other jobs in her agency besides modeling. They also hire receptionists and agents and stylists."

Doreen laughed. "You really checked things out thoroughly for me." She reached for Shanon impulsively and gave her a kiss. "Thanks," she said, taking Faline Trudeau's card.

"Anytime," Shanon said with a blush.

"What's happening in here, girls?" Brad Davis boomed cheerfully. Doreen and Shanon's dad came in the back door from his garage.

"Everything is cool, Daddy," Doreen said brightly. Giving Shanon a wink, she tucked the white card in her pocket.

"Please, Dad," said Amy.

Amy had dropped by at her father's office. She was trying to convince Henry to let her go back to school two days earlier.

"First you complain about what a terrible time you've had over the holidays, then you want to go back early," Mr. Ho said disapprovingly. "The answer is no."

"I never said I had a terrible time!" Amy protested. She bit her lip to keep from saying more. No matter how she felt, she could not bring herself to talk back to her father. She had been taught that saying no to her parents, especially her dad, was disrespectful.

Amy gulped. Her eyes darted furiously around the office. The walls were covered with beautiful hangings and several of her mother's photographs. On her dad's desk was a picture of herself and Alex when they were much younger. Wearing a frilly dress, Amy sat posing demurely. Alex was smiling mischievously and making donkey ears behind her head. Seeing the picture made her fume. All her life things had been this way! Her brother was rewarded for being a "rascal" and she was always expected to be good.

"If Alex were asking to leave home a couple of days early, would you let him go?" Amy asked quietly.

Her father wagged his head. "That brother of yours is such a hothead, he'd probably end up going no matter what we said." A faint smile crossed Mr. Ho's lips. "He's a devil, your brother."

Amy felt her eyes smart with tears. As far as she was concerned, the way her family treated her was totally unjust.

"It was embarrassing to have to go to Max's party with

156

Alex," Amy blurted out, "even though it did turn out all right in the end. I'm fourteen and you treat me like a baby."

"We've been through all this," Mr. Ho said brusquely. He shuffled through some papers.

"Dad, I want to go back to school to make a party for a little boy me and my suitemates have made friends with," Amy pleaded. "He's cute and his family's had a hard time. He didn't have a great Christmas. We want to make a celebration for him and his brothers and sisters."

Amy's dad looked up curiously. "Nice idea," he said.

"I even thought you might even donate some of those small toys the company sells," Amy continued.

Henry got up from his desk. He paced by the window of his office. He looked very pensive.

"All right," he said at last, "you can go back early." He turned to his daughter and gave her a little smile. "This vacation has been a lot of hit and missing, hasn't it?"

"I haven't had a terrible time, really," Amy said apologetically. "It's just that—"

"I get the picture," said her dad. "You want more freedom. Your mom and I have been talking. Maybe we are a little hard on you. If we seem overprotective, it's only because we love you."

Amy gave her father a hug. "Thanks for letting me go back early, Dad!" she said.

Her dad gave her a big squeeze. "Having teenagers is hard," he said. "When you and Alex were younger, it seemed easier."

"That's because you can tell little children exactly what to do," Amy volunteered cheerfully. "When you grow up, you get a mind of your own."

"Alex has always had that!" exclaimed her father with a knowing grin.

"So do I," Amy said. "I need you to listen to *me* sometimes, Dad."

"I'll try, Amy," her dad responded gently.

Amy gave her father a second hug. Even though her dad still hated rock 'n' roll and her ears were unpierced, today she might have made a little progress.

"Thanks again for letting me go back to Alma early," Amy said, flashing a bright smile. "Can I go up to the warehouse and get some of those little toys?"

Her dad grabbed his jacket and smiled. "I'll come, too," he said. He put his arm on Amy's shoulder. "Let's go—daughter!"

Back in Palm Beach, Florida, Palmer Durand was taking a ride with her mom in a shiny red convertible sports car. The day was warm and sunny and the sky was beautiful.

"This is so cool!" Palmer said, letting the wind take her hair. "I love this car. Can we buy it?"

Stephanie Durand chuckled. "I only rented it for the afternoon, my dear. After I got that urgent call that you were coming home and then leaving almost immediately for school, I thought I'd cook up a treat."

Palmer giggled. "A sports car was on my Christmas list, you know. When I saw you drive up in this, I thought it might be a late present."

Stephanie laughed softly. "That's my daughter—wishful thinking!"

Palmer and her mother cruised past the palm-lined waterfront. Basking in pleasure, Palmer sniffed the fragrant air and smiled at her mom. "Nice being in warm weather again," she said.

"Nice seeing you again," Stephanie said, casting her a glance.

Palmer and her mother were nearly look-alikes, both blond and blue-eyed with angular faces.

"You seem a lot more cheerful than you were before Christmas," observed Palmer. "Did you sell one of your paintings?"

"No sales," Mrs. Durand replied over the roar of the motor. "I'm just in a better mood now that the holidays are winding down. Some people get ecstatic over Christmas—I get nostalgic."

"Well, I'm certainly glad you're not depressed any-more," Palmer stated matter-of-factly. "I'm glad to be home with you again, too."

"Thanks for saying so," Stephanie said in a chipper voice. She pulled off the road near the beach. "Want to get some exercise?" she asked.

"Sure," Palmer said. She hopped out of the car, and she and her mother began to stroll along a fancy boardwalk.

"How was L.A.?" Stephanie asked.

"Same-oh, same-oh," Palmer said. "I liked seeing Dad, but I still hate Georgette."

Mrs. Durand wrinkled her nose. "You two never have been the best of friends," she said. "It must be chemistry."

"How was your Christmas?" Palmer asked her mother.

"Lonely," Stephanie admitted. She gave Palmer a squeeze. "It was great getting that second call from you."

"Glad you liked it," said Palmer. "Alicia suggested it."

"Let's not talk about Alicia," her mom said dramatically.

"Sorry," Palmer said with a chuckle. Just like Palmer and Georgette didn't share the right "chemistry," as her mother had put it, Mr. Durand's first and second wives didn't get along either.

"Shall we stop in for tea?" Mrs. Durand asked, indicating a small shop on the boardwalk.

"Sounds great," said Palmer. "I'll tell you all about Max's party."

"There must have been a lot of interesting people there," her mother said.

"Oh, there were!" Palmer bubbled. "First of all I have to tell you about the piano player! He was tall and has dark reddish hair, and his eyes are—"

"What about his music?" Stephanie asked.

Palmer turned bright red. "Oh, th-the music was good, too," she stammered. "Sensational."

A waitress led them to a table. Palmer sat down, blushing. After she'd just blurted things out, she was sure her mother had guessed there was more that she liked about "the piano player" than just his music.

"What's this piano player's name?" Mrs. Durand asked with a mischievous grin.

Seeing the twinkle in her mom's eyes, Palmer giggled. "I hope you meet him someday," she said. "His grandparents have a house in Palm Beach." She lowered her eyes. "He has the most unusual name—Rain. . . ."

"Here's my old dominoes set," Gary volunteered.

"I'm giving a new set of checkers," Brian bragged. "What do you think of that, Bozo?"

"And I'm gonna give my triceratops," lisped Kevin.

Max smiled at her brothers. "Thanks, gang. Just put it in that big box. And don't put any frogs in for good measure," she warned playfully.

"What about a few snakes?" Gary teased.

Max shook a finger. "Don't kid around, doofus. We're supposed to be doing something nice for Jose and the kids in his family, not scaring them to death."

Max's brothers dutifully deposited the toys they were

holding in the large cardboard box in the center of Max's room. Ever since Max and her friends had gotten an okay to go back to Alma early, her whole family had been pitching in to help her. Max wanted to make the party she and her suitemates were planning for the Hurt kids something really magical.

"If only we could get S.C. to make an appearance," Max muttered.

"Old S.C. is probably totally wiped out," joked Gary. "The poor guy works around the clock on Christmas."

"Who's S.C.?" Max's youngest brother Kevin asked curiously.

"Santa Claus, you bozo," Brian said critically. "Don't you know anything?"

Kevin looked puzzled. "Does Santa Claus make personal appearances? I'm talking about the real Santa Claus—not the people who dress up like him, like Dad."

"Maybe," Gary said with a shrug.

"Everybody makes personal appearances," said Brian, "even the President. If you had the right connections, you could probably get Santa Claus."

"The real one?" nagged Kevin. "Or the one at the department store?"

Max smiled. "I'd settle for the one at the department store. Think how thrilled Lila, Billy, and Becky would be," she said, "not to mention Jose."

"Jose's my age," argued Brian. "The way you talk about him, he sounds like a kid."

"He is a kid," Max said, giving Brian a playful rap on the noggin. "Just like you are."

"Ho, ho, ho!" Mr. Schloss announced himself, coming into the room.

"Cut it out, Dad," said Gary, "Christmas is over."

"Okay," agreed Mr. Schloss, "no more impersonations."

161

He raised his hand in mock seriousness. "Scout's honor."

Max rolled her eyes. "Are you ever serious, Dad?"

"Only when I'm snoring," Mr. Schloss joked. He reached into his wallet. "Here's thirty-five dollars, Max."

Max's eyes bugged. "Thirty-five dollars? For what?"

"To help with the party you're giving at the school," her father said.

"Wow, thanks!" said Max. "That'll buy a lot of candy canes! As soon as I get to Brighton, Shanon, Amy, Palmer, and I can go shopping."

"And we've already collected a lot of stuff here," Gary said proudly.

Mr. Schloss peered into the cardboard box and nodded approvingly. "Nice idea you had, Max," he said to his daughter. "I hope your friend Jose has a good time."

"He'll love it!" Max exclaimed. "And so will the other kids. Maggie and Dan thought it was a good idea, too. In fact, they're collecting some things on their own and inviting a few other kids."

"A real post-Christmas event, heh?" Mr. Schloss said, smiling.

"I should say so," said Mrs. Schloss, coming into the room. "It looks like you're going to have one special party, Max."

Max smiled as her whole family stood around talking, joking, and collecting more and more things for the party. It was still a mystery to Max why her family had so much that they could fill a couple of huge boxes with their extras and Jose's family had so little. Max knew that she wasn't going to change the whole world by giving one little party. But it still made her feel good to share some of what she had with Jose. Someday, she would do more, she vowed. Someday when she was grown up and more powerful, she *would* change the world. . . .

162

CHAPTER NINETEEN

Max Schloss's Journal

It is New Year's Eve and the Foxes of the Third Dimension are back in Suite 3-D at Alma Stephens. This afternoon we gave Jose's party. As Amy would say, it was "rad." Even Palmer got a kick out of it, especially when little Becky Hurt decided to name the big walking, talking doll "Palmer." I guess Becky got the idea for the name from the knitted sweater the doll was wearing, but Palmer was thrilled about it anyway. Shanon and her sister gave a whole collection of *Little House . . .* books, which were a real hit with Lila Hurt and I think Jose will take a stab at reading them as well. And Jose loved, and I mean loved, the microscope that I gave him that used to belong to my brother Gary! In a way, now that we are back at Alma I miss the "monster pip-squeaks." Everything seems much too quiet and nothing jumps out of the closet and crawls out from under my pillow. I also miss my mom and my dad a lot. But if you're going to be at a boarding school, Alma is the place to be. Fox Hall is anyway. Maggie and Dan really do make it homey here. If it hadn't been for them, the party this afternoon would not have been as successful or as much fun as it was. Besides the gifts from the Foxes, Maggie and Dan made some wonderful contributions that were gift-wrapped so beautifully. The Fox Hall Christmas tree, though dropping a few needles, was still hanging in there in the common room. And the cookies! Shanon's grandmother and Maggie ought to enter a Betty Crocker bake-off. They'd both win first place. My stomach is still bulging. That's why instead of being asleep like everyone else in the suite, I'm still up. Of course, it also could be all the chocolate chips I hogged down that are making me hyper. I love chocolate chips, especially in brownies, which I ate around twelve of.

Right now I'm thinking of Jose's face when he came into the dorm this afternoon. He is definitely a small kid for nine, and his eyes are enormous and so serious-looking. But his eyes lit right up when he saw the tree and all the nice things for his brothers and sisters. Holidays must be hard for Jose to begin with—the poor little guy doesn't even know his real mother and father, and then his foster family has had so many problems. Maybe today at the party, he forgot that for a while. I still wish there was something permanent I could do for Jose—if I were Santa Claus or some other great spirit like that, I'd give Mr. Hurt a good job and Jose's mom, too. I would give them a permanent house that was big enough for them all so they didn't have to stay in that little trailer. And I would do it all in secret.

In a few minutes, it will be midnight. I guess I will have to wake up Shanon, Amy, and Palmer. We were all going to try to stay up, but those three couldn't make it. Maggie and Dan invited us down to their apartment if we were still awake to see in the New Year. It's really a funny feeling being the only kids in the dorm with the faculty. Mrs.

Butter isn't even in the dining hall! Tomorrow Maggie and Dan are even feeding us. It'll be New Year's Day! I'll make sure to phone Mom and Dad, Gary, Brian, and Kevin. Tomorrow we are also going to give Palmer her prize. Amy, Shanon, and I discussed it and we think that Palmer should get the prize for the longest journal. We agreed that since writing is usually such a chore for Palmer, she really deserves this. So even though Palmer kind of fudged things by writing in big handwriting and making a lot of lists that took up a lot more space than they had to, Shanon, Amy, and I decided to give her a prize. Kind of strange Palmer winning a writing contest—even this way! Just goes to show you what people will do to get a prize. Early this morning when we were shopping in Brighton for Jose's party, Amy found a black dress with thin straps and shiny things on it in the thrift shop. It only cost five dollars, so she sneaked and got it for Palmer. It was probably the one thing on her Christmas list that Palmer really wanted and didn't get and she's got so many clothes she'll *probably* never wear it. But we got it anyway. . . .

Max put down her fountain pen. Stretching her legs, she glanced at the clock and got up from the desk. It was ten minutes to midnight. Glancing around the sitting room, she cleared her throat loudly. Amy was curled up on the floor with a blanket and Palmer was stretched out on the loveseat. Earlier in the evening, Shanon had retreated to one of the bedrooms and hadn't come out. Max went to get her first.

"Hey, Shanon!" she called, stomping into the room. "Wake up!"

Her head slumped forward at her desk, Shanon's billowing light brown hair fell over her face. "Huh?" she grunted with a start.

"It's almost midnight," Max said, shaking her.

165

Rising from the chair, Shanon rubbed her eyes and stumbled forward sleepily.

In the sitting room, Amy was already up. "Good grief!" she exclaimed, grabbing the clock off the desk. "It's almost the new year! Why did you let me fall asleep, Max?"

"How could I stop you?" Max asked mischievously.

Amy put down the clock and shook Palmer. "Hey, Palmer, get up! We're going down to Maggie and Dan's—remember?"

"Where am I?" Palmer murmured drowsily. "Rain . . . Rain . . ."

"I can't believe it!" Amy squealed. "She's talking in her sleep!"

"She's dreaming about Max's cousin," giggled Shanon, sounding a bit perkier.

Palmer's eyes flew open. "Fooled you!" she cried brightly. "I was just fooling!"

"Right!" Max teased. "You were having a heavy dream about my cousin!"

"Or about the weather report!" joked Amy.

A soft knock at the door sent them racing across the room. Amy lunged to open it. It was Maggie.

"Happy New Year!" the young faculty advisor said brightly. Maggie was dressed in her coat, cradling her feisty pet terrier puppy, Gracie. The teacher's violet eyes glowed with merriment. "Hurry outside!" she whispered excitedly.

"Outside?" Palmer said in shock. "It must be freezing."

"Come on," their teacher urged. "Dan's waiting for us!"

Shanon, Amy, and Max threw on their coats. Not wanting to be left behind, Palmer did, too.

"Get some boots on, too," Maggie said.

In a matter of seconds the girls were hurrying downstairs

behind her. There was a hint of magic in the air. Maggie flung open the front door. Above the velvet darkness of the sky was a bright canopy of stars like cut crystal! The lawn was a white carpet of snow.

Dan Griffith stood there grinning. "Let's bring in the New Year," he said, passing out sparklers.

"Sparklers!" exclaimed Amy. "Wow-wee!"

"I thought those were only for the Fourth of July!" Palmer said gaily.

The little group gathered to light their sparklers, then Max let out a whoop and the Foxes were off toward the quadrangle. Crunching through the crusty snow, they ran with their sparklers, making circles and their initials and yelling Happy New Year so loud that it echoed. Returning to Maggie and Dan over and over again, they lit up the night until the little lights in the box were exhausted.

"What a rad night," Amy chuckled as they trudged back inside.

"Another year," Shanon said wistfully.

"Let's go in," demanded Palmer. "I want some hot chocolate."

Max was the last to linger. *I won't forget these stars,* she thought, staring straight up. The lights in New York were bright, but not as bright as these!

MEET YOUR PEN PAL DREAM TRIP SWEEPSTAKES
YOU AND YOUR PEN PAL COULD WIN A TRIP
TO NEW YORK CITY

That's right. The Trumpet Club and Pen Pals are giving you a chance to win a fabulous dream trip to New York City for you, your parent or guardian, your pen pal and your pen pal's parent or guardian.

ENTER TODAY FOR A CHANCE TO WIN!

Here's what one lucky Prize Winner will receive:
A three-day, two-night trip to New York City for you, your parent or legal guardian, your pen pal and your pen pal's parent or legal guardian, consisting of the following:
Round trip airfare (the winner and his/her pen pal must each travel with his/her parent or legal guardian)
Two-night hotel accommodations in New York City (double-occupancy rooms)
Lunch with Sharon Dennis Wyeth, the author of Pen Pals
Tickets to a show
Plus $250 spending money per family
No purchase is required but you and your pen pal must each be a resident of the continental U.S. and between the ages of 8 and 15.
All entries must be received by January 31, 1991.
To enter the PEN PALS DREAM TRIP SWEEPSTAKES complete the Official Entry Form and send your completed entry form to:

THE TRUMPET CLUB
PEN PALS SWEEPSTAKES
100 EAST HOWARD
BOX 41
DES PLAINES, ILLINOIS 60018

PEN PAL DREAM TRIP SWEEPSTAKES
OFFICIAL ENTRY FORM

NAME _____

STREET ADDRESS _____

CITY _____ STATE _____ ZIP CODE _____

PHONE NUMBER _____ GRADE IN SCHOOL _____

DATE OF BIRTH _____

(If applicable, check one) I got this PEN PALS book from

      The Trumpet Club _____

      In a store _____

PEN PAL'S NAME _____

PEN PAL'S STREET ADDRESS _____

CITY _____ STATE _____ ZIP CODE _____

PEN PAL'S PHONE NUMBER _____

PEN PAL'S DATE OF BIRTH _____

Send completed entry forms to: The Trumpet Club
                                       Pen Pal Sweepstakes
                                       100 East Howard
                                       Box 41
                                       Des Plaines, Illinois 60018

COMPLETED ENTRY FORMS MUST BE RECEIVED BY JANUARY 31, 1991

OFFICIAL PEN PALS DREAM TRIP
SWEEPSTAKES OFFICIAL RULES

1. NO PURCHASE NECESSARY.
2. To enter sweepstakes, complete the Official Entry Form and mail it to:

> The Trumpet Club
> Pen Pal Sweepstakes
> 100 East Howard
> Box 41
> Des Plaines, Illinois 60018

To obtain a free official Entry Form, write to Pen Pals Exchange,
c/o Parachute Press, 156 Fifth Avenue Suite 325, NY, NY 10010.
Requests for Entry Forms must be received by January 31, 1991.

3. Any entries that are illegible or incomplete will not be accepted. The Trumpet Club and Parachute Press are not responsible for late, lost, or misdirected entries or for typographical errors in the rules. All entries become the property of The Trumpet Club and Parachute Press and will not be returned.

4. All entries must be received by January 31, 1991.

5. A random drawing will be held on or about February 8, 1991 to select one Prize Winner from all completed entries received. The Prize Winner will be notified by telephone or mail. Odds of winning depend on the number of completed entries received.

6. There is one Prize as follows:

One Prize Winner accompanied by his/her parent or legal guardian, his/her pen pal and the pen pal's parent or legal guardian will be awarded a trip to New York City, which consists of round trip airfare for all four people from airports closest to the winner's home and the winner's pen pal's home, hotel accommodations at a hotel selected by The Trumpet Club consisting of two double occupancy rooms for two nights, lunch with Sharon Dennis Wyeth at a restaurant selected by The Trumpet Club, four tickets to a show chosen by The Trumpet Club, and $250 cash each per family. Both the winner and his/her pen pal must be accompanied by a parent or legal guardian. Airline and hotel arrangements will be handled by The Trumpet Club. The Prize trip package does not include meals (except for the one lunch), ground transportation, gratuities and other incidental expenses. The approximate retail value of the Prize is $4,000, depending on the point of departure of the winner and the winner's pen pal, and on hotel availability. The Prize trip must be taken before August 15, 1991 and dates for the trip are subject to airfare and hotel availability and to Sharon Dennis Wyeth's availability. The winner will be asked to give three alternative proposed dates, and The Trumpet Club will confirm the actual dates of the Prize trip or ask for additional proposed dates to be confirmed by The Trumpet Club. Once confirmed, flight and land arrangements may not be changed or altered by the Prize Winner, the pen pal or the Winner's or pen pal's parent or legal guardian. No substitution or transfer of the Prize is allowed. In the event the Prize Winner or his/her pen pal chooses not to accept his/her prize or the Winner cannot be notified, an alternate winner will be chosen at random from all the completed entries received. The Prize winner is solely responsible for any insurance and any applicable federal, state, and local taxes.

7. Sweepstakes open to residents of the continental United States who are between the ages of 8 and 15 at the time of entry. Employees and their immediate families of The Trumpet Club, Bantam Doubleday Dell Publishing Group, Inc., Parachute Press, Inc., and their subsidiaries and affiliates are not eligible. Void where prohibited by law. The Prize Winner, his/her pen pal and the Prize Winner's and pen pal's parent or legal guardian who will be accompanying the Prize Winner and his/her pen pal on the trip will be required within fifteen (15) days of notification to execute and return any legal documents required by The Trumpet Club, including affidavits of eligibility, promotional release and compliance with official rules. Non-compliance within this time period will result in disqualification and another Winner will be chosen at random.

8. All interpretations of the rules by The Trumpet Club and Parachute Press are final.

9. For the name of the winner available after February 15, 1991, send a stamped, self-addressed envelope, entirely separate from your entry, to:

> PEN PALS DREAM TRIP WINNER
> THE TRUMPET CLUB
> 666 FIFTH AVENUE
> NEW YORK, NY 10103

Residents of Washington and Vermont need not enclose a stamped envelope.

10. Winners agree that The Trumpet Club, Bantam Doubleday Dell Publishing Group, Inc., Parachute Press, Inc. as well as employees of these companies shall have no liability in connection with acceptance or use of the prize awarded herein.

WANTED: BOYS — AND GIRLS —
WHO CAN WRITE !

Join the Pen Pals Exchange and get a pen pal of your own!
Fill out the form below.
Send it with a self-addressed stamped envelope to:

PEN PALS EXCHANGE
c/o The Trumpet Club
PO Box 632
Holmes, PA 19043
U.S.A.

In a couple of weeks you'll receive the name and address
of someone who wants to be your pen pal.

Cut here --

PEN PALS EXCHANGE

NAME _____ GRADE _____

ADDRESS _____

TOWN _____ STATE _____ ZIP _____

DON'T FORGET TO INCLUDE A STAMPED ENVELOPE
WITH YOUR NAME AND ADDRESS ON IT!

Please check one
☐ I bought my book in a store.
☐ I bought my book through the Trumpet Book Club.